to Love a Mate

BESTSELLING AUTHOR

KRYSTAL SHANNAN

Chapter One

Austin, TX
Spring Break, March 2015

It was supposed to be a relaxing week partying with friends, but life was rarely relaxing for Emma Carrington. She leaned against a small steel-topped table and waited for her best friend, probably her only friend, to return from the bar with their drinks. She was in Austin to take in the spring break crowd, relax a little, maybe hook up, and avoid the socialite crap her mother always tried to get her to attend at home in the Hamptons.

"Your friends are getting on my nerves," Hollis grumbled, currently one of the asshole bodyguards assigned to her by her absentee criminal father.

She didn't respond. It didn't matter to her in the least if the girls irritated him or Grimes. It was their job to protect her, not her job to make sure they were comfortable. She was long past trying to be friendly with her bodyguards.

"Here." He set a small bottle of water on the table. "I thought you might want to hydrate between drinks. You were hitting those margaritas pretty hard at the last place."

She looked up at his face and saw nothing. No compassion. No concern. Just a blank stare in his dark brown eyes.

Emma took the water bottle, opened it, and took a small sip.

Hollis flashed her a pretty-boy smile and sauntered off.

Where the hell had that come from? She looked down at the bottle of water. When she'd opened it, the cap had come off without any snapping. The seal had already been broken.

Shit.

She turned away, blocking Hollis's view of the bottle and stuck the tip of her finger in the water. She wore specialty nail polish that changed if exposed to certain drugs—drugs usually found in drinks. Her pink nail polish darkened to black where the water had touched it and her stomach churned.

Had he known? It couldn't be a mistake. Guys like him and Grimes didn't make mistakes. She swallowed nervously, wondering how much the sip she'd taken would affect her.

She grabbed her purse and the water bottle and headed for her friend standing at the bar, doing her best to behave as if nothing was wrong.

"Keely," she leaned close to her friend's ear. The noise of the music in the place would've drowned out her voice otherwise. "I'm going to the restroom and then to the hotel. I don't feel well, but I need you to act like I'm not leaving. I need a head start to get away from Tweedle-Dum and Tweedle-Dee."

They'd played ditch-the-bodyguards often enough for Keely not to be surprised. "Do you want me to meet you somewhere else in a few? You know those other girls will be fine without us," Keely said into Emma's ear.

"No, I need to lie down for a bit."

"Sure. I'll see you at the hotel in the morning," Keely answered with a wink.

Emma forced a smile for her friend's benefit and then headed for the bathroom. First she had to puke. Then she had to find a way out of this blacklight-happy-glow-in-the-dark club without Hollis or Grimes any the wiser.

She waved off Hollis' approach as she crossed the busy dance floor to the bathroom. He nodded and settled into his seat but turned his chair so he was facing the hallway where the bathrooms were.

She ducked into the first open stall, shoved two fingers down her throat, and puked up everything she'd had to drink and eat so far that evening. The taste of bile and stomach acid burned in her throat and mouth, but hopefully she'd gotten whatever had been in that water out of her system fast enough for it not to knock her on her ass. She poured the rest of the water bottle's contents into the toilet and flushed.

When she exited the chrome stall, another chick dressed in tight dark-wash blue jeans, a black lace cami, and a wide-brimmed brown cowboy hat studied her with concern in her eyes.

"Chica, you okay? Need me to call you a cab?" The woman was in her late-twenties, probably a few years older than Emma, but still young enough to find the dirty sixth bars fun.

Emma wiped her mouth with the back of her hand and washed up at the sink. "I'm good, but actually I'm trying to ditch this guy who's harassing me. I'll give you five hundred dollars for the clothes you're wearing right now."

"Five hundred bucks, for this?" The woman pointed to her ragged jeans. "Your shoes probably cost more than that."

"They did. You could easily sell them online for five times what I'm going to give you." Emma smiled. "I really need to get out of here and my clothes glow like a neon sign because of the black lights."

The other chick nodded. "I'm game. Nothing like trying to skip out on an asshole. You got cash?"

Emma opened her purse and flashed the stack of bills she had tucked in her wallet.

Another women entered the bathroom and they fell silent, waiting for her to touch-up her lipstick and pee. When she left, Emma opened the door on the last stall on the line, the handicapped one. The cowgirl stepped inside with her and they stripped down to their underwear.

Emma pulled on the soft jeans, thankful she had enough ass to hold them up. Her double was a little curvier than she was. The boots slid on, a little big, but a nice break from the super high heels she normally wore.

The other woman handed her the cowboy hat

and slipped into Emma's white dress. It clung a little tighter to the other woman's bigger boobs and ass, but it looked good. Her dark auburn hair was about the same length and style too. Hollis wouldn't catch the switch right off the bat with all the crazy strobe lights.

"Switch purses with me too," Emma said, pulling out the contents in her Louis Vuitton and grabbing the fringed leather strap of the other woman's purse.

"That's like a three thousand dollar bag? Are you sure?" The woman's voice squeaked in disbelief.

Emma shoved the designer bag into the woman's hands and nodded. "It goes with the shoes." She dumped the contents of the other woman's bag into the Vuitton and then put her wallet, stun gun, and other necessities in the fringed leather bag. She handed the chick five hundred-dollar bills and slipped the long strap of her new purse over her shoulder.

"Stay here at least another five minutes. Then you can go out. Once he sees it's not me, he'll leave."

"No problem, hon. I've dealt with my fair share of assholes. If he gives me any trouble I'll give him a knee to the nuts."

Emma smothered a smile. She would pay another

five hundred to see this woman knee Hollis in the groin.

"I can't thank you enough." Emma paused at the door and looked at the woman she'd dragged into her mess. She only hoped Hollis and Grimes wouldn't give her too much of a hard time. But she looked tough enough to hold her own. She'd be fine. She had to be.

Right now, Emma had to get as far away from those two as possible. If Hollis was trying to drug her, there's no way Grimes wasn't in on it, too.

She opened the bathroom door and pulled the brim of the hat down a little farther to hide more of her face. She stepped into the middle of another group of women, all wearing cowboy hats too and slowly made her way toward the door, doing her very best not to draw attention to herself.

One glance over her shoulder at Hollis assured her he was still watching the bathroom door, waiting for her to come out. When she turned again she bumped into a guy's shoulder.

"Sorry," she mumbled.

"No problem, miss." The familiar bass voice made her blood run cold.

She nodded, willing herself not to look up. Then pushed through the revolving door and out onto the street. She should've known Grimes would be watching the entrance. Both guards knew she liked to lose them when she went clubbing.

Stumbling out onto the street, she dragged in a deep breath of the humid Texas air and moved quickly to her right, disappearing into a crowd of men and women bustling down the sidewalk. She had maybe ten minutes before Hollis and Grimes wised up.

Her phone chirped from inside the bag at her hip. She pulled it out and felt her heart stop when the alert on the screen said it was from her dad. Swiping the screen, she opened it and started the video message. Her dad's face came on the screen. He was covered in dirt and his nose looked broken. Gunfire popped in the background. She breathed deep and tried not to panic.

"Emma, if you get this message, you need to get to Lucy. I know you can slip your guards. Do it NOW and get out fast. Security has been compromised. If something happens, Lucy will keep you safe. Emma, this is not a drill."

A loud explosion blew from behind, forcing his face to collide with the screen before it went dark. Then the video cut off.

Damn it. Her heart dropped in her stomach. Her

gut telling her if her father wasn't dead already, he would be soon.

Emma frantically dialed her mom's number, almost dropping the phone twice as her shaking fingers tapped the screen, but it went straight to voicemail.

Crap.

She stripped her phone of the colorful pink case. Pulled the battery off and tossed them both into a nearby trashcan. She dropped the rest of the phone to the sidewalk and stomped on it until it broke into multiple pieces.

Continuing down the street, she kept her eyes open for a sewer drain and tossed the pieces of her broken phone down the hole. Protocol dictated that her phone was the first thing she dumped. Next she needed to get to an ATM and withdraw enough cash to last until she got to Lucy's safe house. Luckily she was only about two hours from her destination.

She still had another grand in her wallet, but she needed to grab more before she stopped using her cards, in case something came up. Slipping into a large bar and grill, she looked around the lobby for an ATM. Sure enough, they had one near the bar.

She took out three thousand—her daily limit on

the card. It would have to be enough.

Stepping up to the polished wood bar, she waited to catch the bartender's eye. The tall, tattoo-covered, muscle-bound giant finally nodded his head at her and sauntered over.

"Hey, baby. What can I get for you this evening?"

She forced an easy smile. "I'm actually looking for the nearest car rental place."

"Hmmm, you better call quick. Most of them close at seven. You've only got about fifteen minutes left."

"I've got to get a car. My dad called and my grandma is sick and needs me to come stay with her. I need to get there tonight. Can I borrow your phone for a minute?"

"Sure, sugar." He pulled a cell from his back pocket and unlocked the screen for her.

She did a quick search for car rentals and dialed the one that said it was only a mile and a half away. The line rang three times before a male voice answered.

"Austin Cars, this is Brent, how can I help you?"

"Hi Brent, I need a car delivered right now to Julio's Bar and Grill on Sixth Street. I'll give you two hundred dollars cash if you can get here in less than ten minutes." Emma turned away from the bar, speaking low into the phone to avoid anyone hearing what she was saying.

"I can do that. Do you have a valid driver's license I can take a picture of when I get there? Also I can take a credit card number over the phone and bring the paperwork for you to sign. How long do you need the car?"

"Yes, and I need it for a week." She answered and then recited the long-since memorized credit card number.

"I'll have a blue Chevy sedan outside the restaurant in five minutes."

"Thank you."

She hung up and turned to the bartender. He was watching her with more interest than she was comfortable with. Pulling a hundred bucks from her wallet, she handed it to him along with his phone.

"Thank you for the phone. And, please," she met his inquisitive blue eyes. "I was never here and you never saw me."

He frowned, but took the money and the phone from her hand. "I'm retired army and I can call a cop friend of mine if you need help, sugar. Are you in trouble?"

"I'm fine. I've got a car coming and someone waiting for me," she answered, trying to give him a reassuring smile. Texas men were so protective and friendly, but he had no idea what he was offering to get into the middle of. "Thank you for the offer though."

"Be safe." He slipped the phone and money into his back pocket. "Your secret is safe with me."

She nodded and left the bar, slipping between the crowd of people waiting to be seated just inside the main door and out into the humidity. The air smelled like alcohol and fried food. But at least there was no sign of Hollis or Grimes canvassing the streets yet.

A dark blue sedan pulled to a stop in front of the restaurant's valet service, but the driver waved off the valet. His polo shirt had Austin Cars on the right breast pocket. He'd lived up to her request.

"Brent?" she asked, walking toward him.

"Yes, ma'am. Ms. Carrington?"

She nodded and moved to stand next to him.

"I need a pic of your license, sign this paper, and the keys are yours."

"Thank you," she said, handing him the information along with five-hundred dollars in cash.

"Ma'am?"

"I need the picture of my license to be too blurry to read and you to delete my credit card information. I'm trying to get away from an abusive ex and he will come looking for me."

"I well….We never share our clients' names or information, but it's not really okay for me to accept cash payment—"

She pulled three hundreds out of her purse and tucked them into his hand.

"Not a problem." He snapped a quick picture and showed her the blurry image. "I'll make sure the bill is altered and paid in full with cash. Have a safe trip."

"Thank you."

A few minutes later, she was in the car and driving out of town toward Somewhere, Texas.

She prayed she could get to Lucy before they figured out where she was going.

Chapter Two

Lucy

Somewhere, TX
A month ago…

The store was the same as it was every other day, filled with dozens of little old gray-haired ladies. Most of them rattling on about their grandchildren and the cats, dogs, and flowerbeds that awaited them in their lonely little houses. Hers was filled with military grade weapons, but missing the one little girl she cared most for in the world.

It was depressing to Lucinda Craig. She'd spent most of her life zig-zagging across the world, solving problems most people didn't even know existed. But the best fifteen years of her life had been spent protecting a sweet little girl she'd loved like her own. Then six years ago, without warning, the Carrington family had yanked their daughter away and retired Lucy to a safe house in the middle of Somewhere, Texas. She was a back-up plan that would never be used. It was the same as putting an old horse out to pasture.

Somewhere, Texas wasn't that bad, but she hated that she was now puttering around in a fucking Sac-and-Save twice a week just to get out of the house. She was only fifty-seven. It was embarrassing, but she couldn't leave. If the Carringtons ever needed her, she wanted to be there... for Emma at least.

Maybe one day Emma would need her again.

Maybe one day she could remind that sweet girl how much she was loved.

The way she'd left hadn't been fair to either of them, and she hated Emma's father for shipping Emma off without letting her say goodbye. But Arnold Carrington wasn't a good father. Hell, he wasn't even a good man. That wife of his wasn't much better. Lucinda knew if she hadn't been there for Emma, their daughter would've grown up with nobody but the maids and a few random asshole bodyguards for company.

The rattle of wheels and the appearance of overly large floral patterns disguised as clothing could mean only one thing. The damn pastor's wife had locked in on her position.

Lucinda allowed her gaze to travel upward from the floor. Sure enough, May Geller had come around the corner to join her in the frozen dinner aisle. There was no reason for May to be in the frozen dinner aisle. The hoity-toity bitch from Church Ave. cooked everything from scratch and the whole town knew it—mostly because the asinine woman bragged about it constantly. May was in the frozen dinner aisle to *talk*.

The Lutheran pastor's wife flashed her an artificially large smile and pushed her buggy forward.

God, no.

The last thing Lucinda wanted was to get an earful about how she needed to come to church or bingo night. Or both.

She took a quick step backward, swiveled her buggy and tried to disappear around the corner before May could open her big mouth. It didn't work out though.

The hem of her pants caught on something sharp at the bottom of the shelving unit and she felt her balance falter. She dropped the cell phone she had clutched in her hand and reached up to grab a shelf to catch herself—instead the whole damn thing came down on top of her.

Fuck.

Chapter Three

Somewhere, TX
Spring Break, March 2015

"Grab me a beer while you're in there, would you?" Noah hollered, stretching out on the lounger in front of Kara's pool. He popped the knuckles in his hands and rolled his neck. Nothing helped though. Tension wrapped around his chest, tightening with each passing day.

His fraternal twin brother had moved into her house before Christmas. Luke had been in love with Kara for years, but it'd taken a nearly fatal accident to bring them together. Even though they weren't married yet, they both already sported the magickally induced tattoos around their wrists that marked them as bonded mates. Kara was linked to Luke forever, bound through emotions and physical sensations. Noah could only hope to one day share the same kind of bond.

"Noah, what's with the nervous vibe lately? You act like something's about to jump our and eat you." Kara peered at him from behind her oversized sunglasses. She sipped her corona and waited. Her blue eyes matched the wide Texas sky. "It's a beautiful day. No classes for a week. What gives? I've never seen you this antsy."

The screen door slammed behind them and Noah sat up, taking the bottle from his brother as he passed. Noah laid his hand on his bobbing knee, stopping the movement temporarily. Being still lately, was an issue.

"Mom said you've been sneaking out every night to run," Luke said.

Noah rolled his eyes. Of course his parents knew. Maybe he should've stayed at the frat house, but after Luke moved in with Kara he didn't feel like sharing a room with anyone else. He'd always shared with Luke. Instead he'd moved home and back into his old room.

"I try to be quiet."

Luke sat next to Kara and gave her a quick kiss.

"They're worried about you."

The hair on Noah's neck stood on end. "Is that what inspired this invite? So you could dig around and find out what's *wrong* with me?" He and his brother had always done everything together. Always lived together. Hung out together. He'd always assumed they would find their mate simultaneously, too. It was stupid of him. Love didn't happen on a schedule and, unlike Luke, he didn't have a girl in his life whom he'd been pining over for years.

Still, his wolf had been restless this month. Running every night had been more of a stress reliever than anything.

"Hey, dad is out of town and…" His brother paused mid-lie and changed his tune. "Yes, dad called and said he could feel your anxiety. He wanted to know if you were okay… if he should come home immediately."

"He's coming home tomorrow night. Why didn't he wait to talk to me then?" Noah snapped, his shoulders tensing. Then he slumped, instantly guilty to be taking his frustration out on his brother. "I'm fine, sorry. I feel…I don't know. My magick prickles along my skin constantly and the only way I can get relief is to let the wolf out. So I do, okay.

There."

"Sorry, I'm just doing what dad asked." Luke held up his hands. "So you don't have any idea why your magick feels haywire?"

Noah shook his head. He'd been through stacks of old books about their family history and the curse. The only thing he'd found was that some male werewolves experienced restlessness and agitation before their mate would appear—an early alert system that told them to keep an eye out. But it was inconsistent and rarely documented. No one in their family had ever spoken of it and he wasn't about to tell his brother that he thought his magick was honing on his one his one true mate the way a meteorologist's radar zeroed in on an impending storm. Except that he wasn't expecting a tornado; he was looking for a girl.

Life is so freaking complicated.

He downed the beer and set the bottle on the concrete beside his chair. Pulling off his shirt, he got up and walked to the edge of the pool. Kara had threatened Luke's balls if he tried to throw her in, but to a werewolf the water felt great. The chill was warded off by their supernaturally raised body temperature.

"Don't you dare splash me with that freezing

water, Noah VonBrandt!" Kara screeched, reaching for a towel.

Flashing her a quick grin, he put a hand to the concrete and jumped into the water feet together, barely making a sound and certainly not splashing his brother's mate. The icy cool water washed away the heaviness in his heart and he dipped down, dunking his head under momentarily to wet his shaggy hair.

"It's not that cold, Kara. You should try it."

She snorted. "When the little thermometer says the temperature is out of the sixties, I'll consider it."

"Wimp," he teased.

"Wolf," she shot back, sticking out her tongue.

Luke moved to the side of the pool and sat on the ledge, letting his legs dangle into the water. "You'll tell us if something changes, right?"

Noah took a deep breath and sighed. "Dude, I'm fine. Give it a little time to blow over."

"It's hard, man. It's not like any of us ever get sick."

"I'm not sick. I think it's." He looked away.

"You think it's what? I know that look. You know something." Luke narrowed his gaze.

"I think my wolf is sensing something is coming… or someone"

"A girl?" A wide grin spread over his brother's face.

"Maybe. Leave it be, okay."

"Yeah, yeah. Fine," Luke answered.

"You're gonna tell dad aren't you."

Luke nodded his head up and down slowly. "I have to. He asked me to talk to you. He'll know if I try to keep this from him. Plus, it's not like he's going to be upset that your wolf is looking for its mate."

Noah stared at the two intertwined Celtic knot bracelet tattoos winding around both of his brother's wrists. The magick ink only appeared when the spell was cast and it could only happen once in a lifetime. The curse allowed for one bonded mate and only one. If a mistake was made, a werewolf could wind up pining for the wrong woman for the remainder of his very pathetic life. If his wolf really was sensing his mate's approach, he prayed that lightning would strike or the heavens would offer up some other sign so he would know it was her for sure.

Chapter Four

The city flew by in a blur of neon colored lights as Emma left Austin as fast as she could legally go without risking being pulled over by a cop. Her stomach rumbled, upset it'd lost its dinner. But there was no time to stop and nothing to stop for. The pickings between Austin and Somewhere were sparse and she couldn't risk being caught on camera at a convenience store.

Hollis and Grimes would be able to track her too easily.

She took the main highway out of Austin and headed east. Only having been to Lucy's once before when her mom was kidnapped a couple years ago, she hoped she could find her way in the nearing dark.

The thing with her mom had blown over without incident. Her dad had paid the ransom and her mom had been home the next day. Even so, at least she'd gotten to see her Lucy again. She wasn't allowed to visit. The whole point of having a safe house was to have a place no one else knew about.

When her father had removed Lucy as her bodyguard/caretaker at sixteen, he'd compromised by keeping her on as a safe-house manager who would only be involved if Emma or the family was in danger.

One time in five years.

That was how many times she'd gotten to see the woman who'd practically raised her from infancy. She might have biological parents, but Lucy was the person she considered her mother.

The landscape changed rapidly from city to prairie and then to forest. The highway was dark and filled with those annoying orange construction barrels. Emma had hoped to go faster once she got out of the city, but the construction was slowing her down more than the traffic had. About three hours later, she reached the outskirts of Somewhere.

Who names a town Somewhere, anyway?

She drove through the center of town and exited south onto Farm Road 16. Lucy's place was on the southern outskirts, close to some big ranches owned by a family named the VonBrandts.

Now there was some money that had strangely found its way into a little no-name college town.

VonBrandt Oil Industries, INC was a major player in the American energy industry. They owned rigs in the gulf and natural gas wells all over the Midwest. Mostly she knew them because there were a couple VonBrandt women that had recently married into two of the Hamptons' wealthiest families.

When couples said vows in the Hamptons, their whole life story became gossip for the season.

Funny thing was, the VonBrandt women she'd heard about were pretty boring. Apparently, there wasn't much in the way of gossip when a girl grows up herding cows or baling hay. Both women, Judith and Courtney, had grown up on ranches … in Somewhere, Texas. Their weddings had been the highlight of the season. The headlines had read COWGIRL COUSINS MARRY HAMPTON MILLIONAIRES.

A sign for Farm Road 519 came up on her right and she turned. She thought it was the right road to Lucy's place. As she drove farther, she wasn't so sure. She remembered a white mailbox not long after the first turn.

Damn. All these numbers ran together in her head. She'd passed a left turn a few minutes ago, but it had said Farm Road 516. Maybe that had been it?

A gate came up on her right with the VonBrandt family name spelled out in wrought iron. She didn't remember seeing that when she went to Lucy's before. *Crap.* How the hell was she going to manage a U-turn on this narrow road?

Turning her eyes to the asphalt, she screamed as the car collided with a deer. Airbags shot into her face as the vehicle lurched from the impact. The deer rolled up onto the windshield and crushed the glass. In her panic, she swerved.

The car careened off the road and tipped into the ditch. Everything went sideways and she threw her hands up.

The force of the landing jarred every bone in her body. The shoulder strap of the seatbelt cut into her neck. She groaned, struggling for several minutes to unsnap her seatbelt. It finally released and she pushed open the driver's side door and crawled out onto the grass. Giving up wasn't in her blood, but damn, what else could go wrong today?

She flopped to her back and stared up at the stars

for a few minutes, letting the shock of the impact filter away. The sky was a soft black, twinkling with stars. The night wasn't as dark as she first thought. She could see cleared fields stretching out on either side of the road in the light of the nearly full moon.

It was time to suck it up and figure this out. She was a Carrington. A fighter. If she could navigate years of social torture and rich stuck-up bitches, she could handle finding Lucy's place in the middle of nowhere. This should be easy in comparison.

She crawled to her feet, grabbed her bag, and closed the car door. The road had curled a lot and the shortest way back to Route 16 should be directly across the field she was staring at. Trespassing wasn't at the top of her To-Do list, but it was the middle of the night. No one would see her. The fence was barbed wire, but surely she could get over it without too much trouble.

Finding a place on the fence, she pushed down, but the taut wire didn't have any give. She moved to one of the posts and put her foot on the bottom wire. Maybe it would hold her weight and she could climb over.

With both hands holding the top of the fence post, she carefully found footing. The wires gave a little beneath her weight, but seemed to be holding steady. She got to the middle line and gingerly swung her leg to the other side.

When she tried to maneuver her other leg over, it wouldn't budge. Her jeans had snagged on a barb. She tugged a little harder. Then again. Finally it came loose but her movement was too forced and her momentum made her lose her grip on the fence post. Her left leg dragged across the top line of the fence and she bit back a cry as she tumbled to the ground, landing in a large gooey mound. She picked up her hand and gagged at the smell.

She hadn't landed in mud.

Her leg burned. There was a large rip in the left pant leg of her jeans and a bloody gash stretched down the inside length of her thigh. The bleeding was minimal. She could patch herself up when she got to Lucy's place. Right now she needed to get moving.

"Damn fence."

She clambered to her feet and walked as carefully as she could across the field in the moonlight. As the trees became thicker, the light filtering through the branches was less and less. She picked her way through the trees, stumbling to the ground several times before she got through the first grove. She was filthy. Covered in manure, dirt, and leaves. The boots she'd gotten from the chick in Austin were a little too big and it was really screwing with her balance.

Once through the first grove of trees, she misjudged a step down and slid face first into a shallow ditch or dry stream bed.

"Cow patties and open sky, huh Lucy. Really? You had to move to the Old West? I feel like I should be in an episode of Bonanza or Gunsmoke," Emma growled under her breath, wiping bits of gravel and dirt from the side of her face. The smell of fresh manure hit her nostrils again and she shuddered, searching for the source of the foul odor. Sure enough, her right knee was planted directly in the middle of a large smelly mound.

A vehicle door slammed not too far away and she pulled herself up to the edge of the ditch and peered out. The wind blew gently against her face. She noticed a silver glint not too far away and a man … taking off his clothes?

What the hell?

First the shirt came off, revealing a six-pack that any red-blooded woman would be hard-pressed not to want to lick and rub themselves against like a cat in heat. She certainly would if given the chance. His chest and shoulders were defined, and flexed as he removed his pants too. A grin curled on her lips. He was wearing boxer shorts made from fabric covered in superhero logos. He turned toward the truck to put his clothes in the passenger seat. Then slid his boxers down too, baring a tight muscular ass. Good grief, why weren't there men like this living in the Hamptons? She was constantly surrounded by scotch-drinking golfers or financial investors. And then of course the lawyers who golfed with them.

Damn.

He turned to the side, but still not far enough around for her to really get a good look. But what happened next defied all laws of nature and the real world. He knelt to all fours and his skin shimmered. His head elongated while fur sprouted all over him. Bones snapped, making her cringe, and his body changed from man to wolf. It was done in less than ten seconds, but those moments felt like an hour.

Oh. My. God.

She swallowed a scream and held her breath until the sexy-man-now-turned-wolf loped off into the trees. Her palms were sweating as she reached into her bag for her stun gun before climbing out of the gully. She crept forward on her hands and knees a few steps, keeping her eyes glued to the place where the wolf had disappeared into the tree line. The moon shone down brightly on the open space she was crossing. She prayed he didn't turn around, because he'd be able to see her without difficulty.

She rose to her feet and walked faster toward the big pickup. The cowboy boots were heavy and noisy on the ground, no matter how hard she tried to keep her footfalls quiet. She reached the truck and walked around the front to the driver's side door.

The windows were down and it was unlocked.

She pulled the handle slowly, breathing a sigh of relief when it opened without a sound. Closing it was going to be another matter.

Climbing up into the cab, she checked the ignition. No keys. Her eyes fell on the pile of clothing in the passenger seat. She dug through, pulling his jeans into her lap and feeling through each pocket. The first pocket she checked held a cell phone, but the second held a ring of several keys, including the fob for the truck.

Holding her stun gun in one hand, she put the fob in the ignition with the other and turned it. The huge vehicle roared to life. Its headlights and overhead lamps cut a bright swath through the darkness ahead of the truck.

Shit. If he didn't hear me, he'll definitely see me.

She glanced in the rearview mirror in time to see him running toward the truck… every gorgeous naked inch of him. Slamming the door shut, she locked it and hit the button to roll the windows up.

"Hey!" he shouted, yanking on the door handle. "What the hell?"

She reached for the shifter, but her hand swooped through empty air. Where the hell was it? She looked at the dash again.

His fist connected with the window and glass shattered all over her lap.

"Noooooo," she screamed, as his hand felt around for the tab to unlock the door. She pushed the button on her stun gun and it sparked to life. She pressed it to his neck and a terrifying growl rumbled from within him, making her heart pound faster. No way was wolf-man getting her out of this truck.

"Sonofabitch," he muttered, staggering backward and dropping to his knees on the ground.

Turning to the dash again, her gaze alighted on a round knob, like a stereo dial, that turned for the gears. She punched the break, turned the dial to D, and then hit the gas. The truck leapt forward and she plowed through the grass until she came out on a dirt and gravel road. She turned and followed it in the direction she'd come. A few minutes later she was at their gate.

She pulled to a stop and jumped out to open the massive steel barrier. It swung wide and she hurried to the truck. Following the farm road, she finally reached 16 again and headed for the turn off she'd passed on the other side.

Chapter Five

A few minutes later, Emma spied the white mailbox she'd missed the first time down the road. Yanking on the steering wheel, she turned down the narrow driveway. The back end fishtailed, but caught the ground a second later. She stomped the gas pedal and did her best to stay on the long gravel driveway. Gravel pellets hit the inside of the wheel wells like hailstones in a storm.

Panic surged through her chest. Breath was difficult to draw. All she wanted was to find the safety of Lucy's house. She would know what to do. Where to go.

The whitewashed old farmhouse came into view and she sighed, relieved. Soon. Soon she would be leaving with Lucy and heading out of the country until her parents could sort out this latest mess.

Her father refused to stop doing business with less than upstanding individuals and so their family continued to pay the price. Hopefully the cost for this debacle wouldn't include someone's life.

She'd almost lost her mother last year.

Arnold Carrington had promised to stop doing dirty deals after that incident, but it was apparently too much to expect him to follow through with such a promise. Now both of her parents were missing and her bodyguards were part of it. *Bastards*.

She followed the driveway around to the back of the house. Putting the truck into park, she slipped out and walked to the large sliding barn door. After a couple of yanks, it whined and started to slide open. She pushed it halfway and then ran to the truck.

Once it was parked out of sight, she tugged the door closed.

Lucy's house stood before her, dark and uninviting. It was strange. She would've thought the noise of the truck would've roused the battle-hardened woman. Nothing got past Lucy.

Emma climbed the steps onto the wide wraparound porch and knocked gently on the back door.

The sound echoed through the stillness of the night. An owl hooted from the trees standing to the right of the house. A shiver danced up and down her spine and she knocked again.

"Lucy? It's Emma."

Still no answer. All manner of terrifying thoughts ran through Emma's mind. What if Lucy didn't live here anymore? What if she was gone? What if they'd gotten to Lucy already? She could be lying dead in the house and no one would know.

Bile rose, burning her throat, and she pressed her hand over her mouth. She frowned and moved away from the door.

Maybe she was sleeping.

Emma followed the porch around to the front door and froze in place as her eyes alighted on a large stack of newspapers. Had to be close to two dozen or more lying against the base of the front door on the welcome mat.

Shit.

She hurried around to the back door again and took a deep breath before using her elbow to bash in one of the panes of glass. It shattered with a loud crash and she winced, hoping no one had been close enough to hear it. At least no alarms had gone off in the house yet. But when she'd visited before,

Lucy said there wasn't a system built into the house. No, the alarms had been placed around the artillery storage upstairs and in the floor cellar beneath the staircase.

Reaching through the broken pane, she unlocked the door and let herself in.

"Lucy?" She called out quietly, still hoping in the back of her mind that Lucy would magically appear out of thin air. That the ignored newspapers meant nothing. Now that she thought of it, Lucy's old Cadillac was missing from the barn and driveway as well. Still, she clung to the hope that everything was going to be okay. Lucy always made everything okay.

Lucy had been forced to retire as her nanny when Emma turned sixteen. Her parents were tired of her. Or at least that's the better version of the lie Emma told herself. She'd been sent to Montpelier School for Girls and Lucy had been put out to pasture in Somewhere, as a safe house keeper for the family should there come a time one was needed.

Well, Emma needed her now and Lucy was nowhere to be found.

"Lucy," she hissed, moving toward the staircase. She climbed to the second floor and wandered through each room.

The house was empty.

Emma sniffed the air and grimaced. The stench was coming from her. Showering was a necessity, finding out where Lucy was could at least wait that long. Her clothes were covered with grass stains and manure. She smelled like a horse stall that hadn't been cleaned in a week.

Flipping on the hall light, she looked around for the linen closet she remembered seeing last year. She opened a narrow door at the end of the hall and pulled down a couple of large white towels from the top shelf. A bottle of tangelo scented shampoo sat on the bottom shelf and she grabbed that too, just in case.

She walked through the guest room where she had stayed previously and into the adjoining bathroom. Everything Lucy had bought her last time was neatly arranged on the counter. Ready and waiting for her return.

She sniffed and wiped her nose with the back of her hand, trying to blink away the tears welling in her eyes. All of this was for her and neither of them knew if they would ever see each other again. Dropping the towels on the counter, she flipped on the water in the shower and waited for it to steam before stepping into the claw foot tub and pulling closed the surrounding curtain.

The water hit her skin like a branding irons. But the pain from the scalding water helped her temporarily forget the encroaching nausea and the fear of being stuck in Somewhere without Lucy. The next closest safe house was in Colorado. She'd have to use her credit cards to buy a ticket and there was no way the security detail wouldn't pick up on that. At least with the rental car, she hoped the cash payment would slow them down. Not that they wouldn't eventually figure it out and then track the GPS in the rental car. It actually worked to her benefit that it had crashed several miles from Lucy's place. Maybe it would give her a little longer to sort out her next move. That was if they didn't know about Lucy's place already. Which they probably did.

Rinsing the last bit of grime from her hair and skin, she turned off the water and climbed out of the tub. After wrapping her long hair in one towel, she used the other to wrap her body.

The dirty jeans and cami stared at her from the white tile floor of the bathroom. Hopefully Lucy had kept some of the clothing she'd bought when she was here last. Otherwise she'd have to find the washer and dryer pronto.

She hurried through the nippy bedroom and yanked open the top drawer of the antiqued red dresser. *Thank God.*She snatched a pair of panties, yoga pants and a t-shirt that said "Save a Horse, Ride a Cowboy" from the drawer.

After pulling on the soft spandex and knit, she went to the bathroom to comb out and dry her wet hair. It'd been hours since she'd eaten, but she refused to soak the back of her shirt because she was too lazy to dry her hair.

Thirty minutes later, she sank into the big black leather couch and turned on the TV while she gobbled down a peanut butter and jelly sandwich and a handful of pretzels. It wasn't what she was used to, but it would have to do for now. Besides, there was something comforting about a peanut butter sandwich. It helped her forget that she was most likely being hunted by armed, military-trained thugs bent on kidnapping and ransoming her.

And then to top it off, there was the added stress of the man/werewolf she'd spotted just down the road who was probably pretty pissed off about being electrocuted and truck-jacked.

The day really couldn't get much worse. At least she hoped not. *And since when are werewolves a real thing?*

The news droned on about gas prices and political candidates, but it was better than sitting in silence. Then a bulletin popped up that made her heart race in her chest. She pressed the button on the remote to turn up the volume.

Wealthy New England family, Arnold and Erika Carrington and daughter Emma, were reported missing today after failing to attend a charity brunch the couple had personally organized. Police have no leads and are asking anyone with information to come forward and call the family's personal security line. Their twenty-one year old daughter, Emma Carrington, has also been reported missing by friends she was traveling with in Austin, Texas.

Her fingers dug into the arm of the couch and she gasped for air, not even realizing she'd been holding her breath.

The news station showed a short clip of one of her father's security officers asking for anyone to call if they had information. A photo of her parents and a photo of her was also shown briefly as the same security officer continued to explain that they were waiting on ransom calls while they continued to investigate the disappearance of all three.

Bastard. He's probably in on it too.

After her stomach stopped threatening to abandon her body, she would take a few minutes to look around the house for weapons, Lucy's computer, and the stash of cash and passports.

She needed to be prepared for the possibility that they'd already gotten to Lucy. Emma's hands shook as the reality of the situation hit her. At any moment, she could be facing armed mercenaries or a pack of werewolves. She definitely needed a gun. Probably several.

Chapter Six

"Ughhhhh," Noah groaned. He rolled to the side and winced as rocks and sharp grass poked into his skin.

Damn it. He rubbed his neck and hissed when his fingers grazed the spot where the stun gun had burned his skin. It would be gone in a few hours, but for now it hurt like someone had jabbed him with a hot iron.

He opened his eyes and took a deep breath. He could still smell her scent on the air, whoever she was. What really wouldn't let his heart slow was the realization that she'd seen him change. She knew he was a werewolf. He was always so careful. But, the little blonde had been covered in manure and downwind. She had to have been on foot on their land. No one in town would purposefully trespass on the ranch, much less in the middle of the freak'n night. Even more disturbing was the way his magick had pulsed around him when he'd approached the truck and smashed the window. It was like the fact that she'd been stealing her truck wasn't even an issue. He'd only wanted to touch her. It was still the only thing he wanted to do.

"I'm so fucked." Noah shook his head and shivered as magick coursed through his body again, changing him at the cellular level. Everything ached from the shock of her Taser, but a moment later he was on four paws and running as hard as he could.

The cool night air whipped through his fur. He took the long way around so he didn't spook the small herd of cattle grazing south of his parent's house.

He trotted up to the side entrance and barked. Sneaking in wasn't an option since his clothes and his keys were in the truck.

A moment later a light flooded the dark walkway and the door opened to reveal his mother with a you've-got-to-be-shitting-me look on her face.

"Why the hell are you barking at the door at three am?"

Noah whined and slunk through the open

doorway.

"Get your furry ass upstairs and put on some clothes. Your father and I will be waiting in his study. You have some explaining to do." His mother growled at his retreating form and slammed the door behind him. "You know I don't like wolves in the house."

He tried to hurry, but he couldn't get traction on the hardwood and ended up halfway skidding across the room before he was able to turn and make a dash for the staircase. The rug on the stairs made the climb a cinch and he was inside the room his twin brother and he used to share. Now it was all his.

Noah stretched and called the magick, shivering again as it prickled across his skin like thousands of insects crawling. His bones cracked and shifted. Standing from his crouched position, he grabbed some clean clothes from the dresser and sighed.

This was not going to be a fun conversation. After pulling on the clothes, he sat on his bed and grabbed the house phone from its stand. He pressed #1 and waited.

"What the hell, Noah?" A familiar deep and groggy voice rumbled over the line.

"I need you at the house. I've got a problem."

"What happened?" Luke's voice changed from lethargic to worried instantly.

"Some chick saw me shift out in the south pasture. She stole my truck and took off."

"How did you let a human get away from you, Noah!?"

"Look, dude, she Tasered me out of nowhere. By the time I was able to move again, she was gone." His face heated. His brother was right. No human should've been able to get the one up on him. But that little slip of a girl had and it was rubbing his fur the wrong way. He didn't need Luke giving him hell too.

Noah heard Kara asking what was wrong in the background.

"Tell Kara I'm sorry for waking her up. Can you guys head this way in a little while? I can find her, I just have to turn on the locator on my phone."

"Sure," Luke sighed. "Kara is already getting dressed."

"Thanks, man. I gotta run, I can hear Mom and Dad arguing downstairs already."

His brother grunted and Noah replaced the receiver on its bay. It was time to figure this out. *Damn it to hell.*

He took the stairs two at a time and traipsed

across the house toward his father's study, following the sound of his mother and father's worried voices. His heart sank at the sound of their disappointment. If it wasn't already bad enough, his uncles were there as well. *Damned cameras.* They were a necessary evil, but such an invasion of privacy.

The VonBrandt family had existed in Somewhere since its founding and only three times in history had a VonBrandt wolf exposed their secret to a human by accident. They were so careful. So private. However with technology becoming more and more advanced, it was only getting harder. But tonight…it never should've happened.

"Noah," his mother called out from inside the study.

He pushed the heavy oak door open and stepped inside. Tonya VonBrandt was pacing in front of the large fireplace while his father sat behind his desk nursing a glass of bourbon. Uncle Adam and Allan were on the couch with their arms folded across their chests. *Shit.*

"Is she a local?" Adam asked, his deputy sheriff badge glistening from its place on his belt.

Noah shook his head, glancing up at the monitors behind his dad's desk that were playing his mistake on loop. "I don't think so. I've never seen her before. Doesn't mean she doesn't live here though." He took a breath and tried to calm the overwhelming urge he had to tell them he thought she was the reason he'd been so agitated lately. But he knew better than to throw that in the mix of this mess right now.

"True," his father added.

"We have to call Siobhan and her sister, Katherine. This woman is already in the wind and could tell any number of people before we find her. The situation must be handled quickly," his mother said, grabbing an iron from the hearth and jabbing it at the burning logs in the fireplace.

The fury behind her strikes was all the hint Noah needed. He had to move fast or this chick was as good as erased. His chance at happiness would be erased with it, if he was right.

"Tonya, breathe. We aren't that far yet. First we need to find out what's going on with her. There may be more than a wolf sighting to deal with," Allan said.

"We found her wrecked rental car close to the ranch's main gate. She has no luggage and the rental's registered papers said Austin."

Noah swallowed. Why was this girl out in the middle of the night, driving in from Austin?

"Look, my phone is in the truck. Let me find her and bring her back to the house. Maybe we can still contain the situation without bringing in the witches. Or anyone else." He took a step backward and reached for the door handle behind his back.

"Noah." The ice in his father's voice made his blood thicken in his veins. "You know there's only two outcomes to this scenario. Only a mate bond would prevent her from betraying our family. She saw you. Our laws stand."

Noah took a deep breath and nodded. "Give me a little time before you call them. She deserves a chance."

"What about you?" his mother cried out. "If you take on this responsibility, you lose your only chance to bond with your future wife. This isn't something you just use to get yourself out of a problem. It's a permanent link to a person. It will create an emotional link that will keep her from outing us, but she's still a stranger."

His mom's words made sense. But he couldn't allow his family to steal this girl's life away from her without exhausting every other option first. She'd fought so hard to get away from him and hadn't fallen into hysterics after seeing him change. Instead, she'd stolen his truck and electrocuted him.

She wasn't an average girl and he sensed that she needed help. His gut said she wasn't a threat, either. Bond or no bond. But the pulse of magick he'd felt when he was near her confirmed in him mind that she was important, possibly the one he'd been waiting for.

Now he had to convince his family.

"Find her before the sun rises, Noah. If she slips away, we will have to call the hunters. If that happens, there won't be a choice for her or for you." The finality of his father's words should've hit his gut like a ton of bricks, but he couldn't stop thinking about the terrified little blonde who had knocked him on his ass.

There was something in her demeanor...she'd been scared out of her mind when she'd taken his truck, but there'd been a quiet strength, too. She hadn't become hysterical. In fact, she'd been so in control that she'd been able to surprise him and use that blasted Taser on him before he knew what was happening.

"I'll find her." Noah yanked open the door and ran across the hall to their family library. His laptop sat open on the large table in the center of the room. A minute later, he had the locator turned on and shook his head in disbelief. His phone was less than five miles away on old lady Craig's land, a quick jog up route 16.

He practically flew out the back door toward the stables. The horses wouldn't appreciate being awakened in the middle of the night, but he could get there a lot faster and quieter if he took a horse instead of a car. Changing into a wolf and running there wasn't really an option unless he wanted to talk to her naked again.

The idea of seeing her naked had crossed his mind, but he really preferred to introduce himself clothed the second time he ran into her.

Ten minutes and several sugar cubes later, he had a gelding named Copper saddled and ready to go. He took off down the dirt roadway toward the east fence. There was a small gate straight ahead on farm road 16. He could use that to get off of the ranch.

The horse gave his all and they quickly crossed the smaller front half of the ranch and slipped through the gate to the farm road. Noah moved Copper off to the west side of the road where there was no ditch.

A few minutes later, he turned his horse and slipped through a stock gate onto Lucinda Craig's land. He didn't really want her to see him coming, so he circled around to the back of the property.

He slowed the gelding's gait to a walk as he approached the big white farmhouse that everyone in Somewhere knew not to visit—ever. Lucinda Craig might be a reclusive middle-aged lady who didn't like anyone, but she was also known for being cranky and a crack shot. Nobody really knew much about her and the only person she allowed on her land without harassing him was Glen the mail carrier.

Fortunately for Noah, he knew the old lady was laid up in the hospital from a serious accident in town a couple weeks ago. Still, if this girl was related to Lucinda Craig, she could be just as dangerous. He already knew she carried a kick-ass Taser. He imagined that being struck by lightning hurt less than that sucker had.

Chapter Seven

Noah dismounted and tied Copper securely to a tree out of sight of the house.

Keeping to low brush and scrubs, he made his way toward the barn. His truck wasn't out in the open, so she had to have stashed it inside.

He glanced at the house again, but only one light was on in the house, illuminating an upstairs window. Other voices from inside made him suspicious of a radio or television as well, so he couldn't be sure exactly where she was.

The girl's scent filled his lungs. His magick pulsed around him, stronger this time, nearly knocking him off his feet. He pushed against the barn door and grimaced when it creaked like a floorboard in a horror movie just before the ax came down to chop someone in half.

He froze, waiting to see if she would emerge from the house. No one came out and nothing changed on the inside.

He pushed again and slipped between the large sliding door and the wall of the barn. The smell of grease, fuel, and old hay filled his lungs. The inside of the barn was pitch black. He narrowed his eyes and called up his wolf, allowing his animal side to enhance his eyesight enough to see.

Sure enough, he could now make out the outline of his truck directly ahead of him. He moved along the side of the vehicle and pulled open the passenger door. His clothes were still lying on the seat. Digging through the pockets of his jeans, he retrieved his phone, wallet, and pocketknife. Then he maneuvered silently to the door and pushed it open enough to slip out into the moonlit early morning.

In an hour or two, the sun would show its face over the forest horizon and sneaking around was going to become exponentially more difficult. He needed to get her to the estate before the town started to wake up. Even though Allan was a deputy, raising questions in town was not something they could ever afford, even if it meant taking drastic measures.

The pack must be protected. That's why there were live-feed security cameras all over the hundreds of acres the family owned.

Allan could only smooth out so much without raising eyebrows. Sheriff Randall might play the part of a good ol' country boy, but he had a nose for secrets that no one wanted to alert.

Moving slowly, he crossed the yard to the porch. There was nothing to hide him, so he could only hope she wasn't watching out the window and as trigger happy as Lucy was

Nothing happened.

He climbed the porch stairs to the back door. A window was broken in the door, and the sight left him frowning. If she was supposed to be here, why break in? Except Lucy wasn't home and a visitor from out of town might not know she was in the hospital.

His family only knew because of Allan. Being a deputy in a small town came with perks—one being Edna's wagging tongue. That old secretary knew everything that happened to everyone in town.

Noah reached for the doorknob and pulled. It clicked and swung open. He stepped cautiously into the kitchen and closed the door. Her scent permeated this room as well and her unsteady breath sounds came from the other side of the kitchen, but he couldn't see her. Where the hell was she? He held his breath and listened for her heartbeat.

Before he locked onto it, the squeak of a door hinge behind him gave away her location. He turned toward the tell-tale squeak and almost immediately collided with something moving fast and hard. Pain radiated through his face. His nose crunched and he stumbled backward, tripping over his own feet and groaning as his ass hit the hardwood.

"Damn! You've got to stop attacking me." He tenderly touched his broken nose and wiped blood from his mouth. That was going to hurt for hours.

"Oh, God! You're the naked wolf-man! Why are you here?" She stood over him, brandishing an iron skillet, reminding him of the animated Rapunzel character from that movie a few years ago. At least he was still conscious and her hair wasn't long enough to tie him up in. Not that he would mind being tangled up in her gorgeous hair.

Damn she was hot. Legs that stretched for miles and breasts that he couldn't help but want to touch. Her nipples were tight beneath the little t-shirt she was wearing, teasing his eyes with their delightfully perky peaks.

"Are you checking me out while your bloody nose runs all over the floor?"

Heat flamed up his neck and onto his face.

"Look, you're the one who stole my truck and Tasered me, by the way."

"I watched you turn into a wolf."

Noah held up his hands, letting her know he wasn't armed. He didn't see another weapon on her, but there was no need to take a chance. The woman could apparently wield a skillet as well as she could a Taser. He was going to hazard a guess that she might have a clue about how to operate a firearm too.

"Still doesn't give you the right to go around stealing cars and knocking people out."

"You were a wolf. You didn't need the truck at that moment. And I didn't Taser you—it was merely a stun gun," she repeated, still staring at him. Her body was visibly tensed and the pan was raised, ready to strike again at the slightest provocation. "How did you find me?"

"My phone was in my pants and I don't give a shit what it's called. That sucker hurt."

She raised an eyebrow, narrowing her gaze at him, a flash of confusion showing in her shining blue-gray eyes.

"I went home and turned on the locator. My phone was in the truck you stole," he explained further.

"Shit. Who else knows where I am?"

"Nobody yet, but it won't take long for them to track me if I don't get you to my house."

"And why would I want to go to the house where a wolf-man lives? Where people are waiting for me? You're obviously used to dealing with dumb blondes. I assure you, I don't fall into that category."

"I don't think you're dumb. I'm just worried about which weapon you might use to assault me with next."

The slightest smirk turned up the corners of her full lips.

Noah held back another groan and climbed to his feet, keeping his hands out away from his sides.

She took a couple steps backward and put the pan down on the counter. "Are you going to call the police about your truck?"

His mouth threatened to drop open. With everything that had happened, everything that she'd witnessed, she was worried *he* was going to call the police?

"Hadn't crossed my mind. I've got more at stake than a truck." He shoved his hands into his jean pockets and took a step closer. She wasn't going to come willingly and he hated putting his hands on a woman without consent, but he had to take her back with him. If she didn't, others would come for her and they wouldn't be nearly as sympathetic.

She countered his movements by backing up again and moving around the island in the center of the kitchen. It was a good plan, especially if he'd been human. But a few extra steps of a head start wasn't going to help her get away from him a second time. Still, he had to give her points for effort.

The rumble of an engine from the driveway pulled her focus from him and he lunged, but she'd already started running.

Shit. She was a quick little thing.

He turned to run after her but she hadn't gone far and was flanking the front window, peering outside between the curtains while keeping her body safely tucked behind solid wall—like she expected to be…shot at?

"Who are you?"

"Shhhhhh," she hissed. She turned to him for a second. "Get down. I don't want them to know I've seen them."

"Who?" Noah asked, even more curious now.

She jerked her thumb over her shoulder and walked to the closet door below the staircase. "Come on."

He frowned and walked to the window instead. Two men were getting out of a black SUV and carrying automatic rifles in their hands. *Holy shit!*

"Who the bloody hell are you?" he growled under his breath. *And who is Lucy?* He pulled the curtain into place and hurried toward her.

She turned to face him and he gulped. An automatic rifle was slung over her back and she was fastening a shoulder holster over her head into which she shoved a Ruger .357.

Squatting to the floor, she pulled a few more things out of a hole in the floor of the closet and shoved them into what looked like a fringed western purse.

"Here."

He took the pistol from her outstretched hand and drew in a deep breath. He'd never shot at a person before and didn't want to now.

"You smell like a horse. Is it tied up nearby?"

Noah's eyes widened and he nodded, shocked by how calmly she was dealing with this situation. Like it was normal. Like people with automatic weapons showed up every day in her life.

Beams of light flashed across the room, filtering through the thick curtains. Images of her bloody and dying on the floor of the house flashed through his mind and his heart raced. He clenched his hands into fists and pulled in another deep breath to calm himself.

"We've got to get out of here." Noah grabbed her hand and made a dash for the back door.

He pulled the door open and they slipped through as a loud crash shook the bones of the house.

"Lucy is gonna be pissed if they tear up her house," the girl grumbled under her breath. "I'm gonna kill Hollis and Grimes if they did anything to her."

Noah yanked her hand. "Shut up and follow me. Lucy is in the hospital in town."

"What?"

Her heartbeat raced and he could smell the change in her mood shift almost instantly. Sweat beaded across her forehead and her palm slicked in his hand. She'd gone from being calm and collected to insecure and terrified.

Shit.

"Now," he roared, yanking her along behind him. His palm hit the back door with a thud, sending it flying open as he pulled her out and down the steps to the backyard. For a moment he considered grabbing her around the waist and carrying her to where the horse waited in the shadows of the tree line, but she was surprisingly nimble on her feet and kept up with his rushed pace.

He slid to the ground and ducked behind some shrubs, vaguely aware that his hands were all over very curvy parts of her body as he tried to hide them both from view behind scraggly wild privets.

"Watch it," she hissed under her breath, but didn't move away from the shelter of the greenery.

She wasn't stupid. That was for sure.

He pulled his hands slowly from her ribcage and kept his gaze glued to the doorway. A big burly guy in a black suit walked through the open back door and surveyed the yard.

"She was here," the man shouted over his shoulder. "The fucking door is still swinging and the TV is on."

Another volley of curses filtered out from inside the house and the burly guy went inside after one more perusal of the yard.

Noah detected the slightest shudder run through

the small female next to him on the ground.

"What's the plan wolf-man? I've got guns, but Hollis and Grimes are just as good at shooting as I am. Probably better, because they get more practice."

His chest tightened and he looked over at her, narrowing his gaze. "You *know* those assholes carrying automatic weapons?"

She nodded. "They were my bodyguards until about six hours ago. I didn't think they'd figure out where I went so quickly. The dumbasses are smarter than I gave them credit for. Lucy would've known what to do."

"Why would old lady Craig know what to do with crazy bodyguards turned evil? Why are they chasing you?"

"Money," she murmured. "I'm pretty sure they've killed my parents already. They figured it would be easier to get me to give them money than ask for ransom."

Noah's mind spun with the overload of information. Who was this girl? If she was someone with a lot of money who people would miss, his father's idea of giving her amnesia was not going to go very smoothly. In addition, his magick was was pulsating, translating his wolf's excitement over their close proximity into an urgent desire to have her even closer.

And how was she not more upset about her parents supposedly being killed? If his parents were missing or presumed dead, he'd be a wreck. Although, she had seen him change into a wolf and kept her wits about her enough to electrocute him with that stupid-ass stun gun.

"Look, we have to get to my house. There are things that need to be discussed and—"

"Look wolf-man, all I need to do is get to Lucy and get out of town. Then we can both go back to living our lives like none of this shit ever happened." She drew her legs up under her body, as if she were preparing to take off running into the trees.

"It's not that simple, and where do you think you're going?"

"Town. You said she's in the hospital."

"The only way in and out of this piece of property is down that driveway or through the stock gate where I came in." He got to his feet, but stayed low behind the shrubs. "Come on. I've got a horse this way, behind those oaks," he said, pointing to his left.

"Geez, finally."

The next instant millions of volts of electricity coursed through his body and he bit back a shout of anger.

Sonofabitch. That hurts. And on the neck again.

He cringed from the ground as he watched her slink off in the direction he'd pointed. The nerves in his body felt as though he'd plugged them into a giant wall socket. Pain seared along his right shoulder and arm. His muscles spasmed and he struggled to move his arms and legs. She must've turned the juice up on that thing from the last time. Through sheer force of will, he climbed to his feet and limped after her.

He had to get to her before she got to Copper.

Chapter Eight

Emma tucked the stun gun into her bag and sprinted through the trees where the guy had pointed. She saw the horse standing calmly, tied to a low hanging branch.

"Thank goodness for riding lessons." Still, even with Ms. Gregor's years of lessons, she was dressed for a yoga class, not riding western in the dark through forested terrain. It'd been hard enough driving that monster of a pickup truck out of the VonBrandt field, up onto the road, and then down the narrow driveway to Lucy's house. The only thing she drove at home was her small Beamer.

A heavy hand clamped down on her should and she turned, instinctually throwing a punch, but a second hand caught her fist. She found herself face-to-face with a really pissed off wolf-man. She wriggled her hand, but he didn't loosen his vice-like grip.

"Use that thing on me again and I will knock you out and carry you like a sack of potatoes. Do you understand me? I don't usually hit girls, but two electrocutions in one night is wearing my patience very, very thin."

She flexed her muscles again, but nodded her head. Now wasn't the time to negotiate. They needed to get as far from Hollis and Grimes as humanly possible. Hell, she didn't even know where the damn hospital in this town was. For now she might as well stick with this guy until a better option arose.

"Are we getting out of here or what?" she asked, motioning to the empty saddle.

He finally released her shoulder and she winced as blood rushed to the area he'd compressed with his fingers. The guy was strong and a little scarier than she'd first thought. Still, he had kind eyes and that wasn't something she was used to seeing in her circle of associates.

"Let's go." He swung up into the saddle and extended his hand. "But leave the guns here."

"I'm not leaving myself unarmed with those guys

creeping around God knows where after they finish searching the house for any trace of where I went."

"Rifle. Ground." He pointed to the pine needle-covered soil at her feet.

She huffed, but laid the large assault rifle down before taking his hand. At least he hadn't balked at the handgun holstered to her left side.

He pulled her up behind him on the horse like she weighed nothing. Then guided her hands to his waist and patted them.

"Keep your hand here, so I know you're not planning another sneak attack with that damn Taser."

"Stun gun."

"Whatever." His voice was gruff, but she detected a hint of amusement.

She tightened her hold around his stomach, her arms grazing the top hem of his jeans. Beneath her fingers was a body of hard-core muscles. She knew that already from her peek at him naked earlier tonight, but she hadn't truly appreciated it until now as she clung tightly to his rock hard abs.

A few minutes later, the only thing she could focus on was the jarring sensation of the horse's rump colliding with hers on every step. It felt like she was riding shallow rapids without a raft. Up and down. Up and down. *Ugh.*

When they finally got to his place, she wouldn't be able to walk on her own and her ass would look like a Jackson Pollock painting from all the bruises. Not to mention the yoga pants were going to reek of horse sweat.

Luckily, Hollis and Grimes seemed completely oblivious to the fact that she'd slipped right out the back door. If she could find out what was going on with Lucy, maybe she could still get away before those double-crossing assholes took what they wanted from her and left her for dead in some abandoned back alley in this redneck town. These rich cowboys certainly weren't going to be any help against trained guns. Although…the wolf-man-thing made her wonder what else her victim-turned-rescuer was hiding.

"Do you know what happened to Lucy?"

"The poor woman accidentally tripped on a display in the local grocery store. She bumped her head really hard and, as far as I know, hasn't woken up yet. I think it has been a couple of weeks."

"She's unconscious?" Emma's heart stopped in her chest and breathing was suddenly painful. What was she going to do without Lucy? She had no idea how to go about avoiding Hollis and Grimes without help. She'd been trained in weapons by Lucy, but everything was at the farm—with Hollis and Grimes. All she had was the hand gun and every spare clip she could fit in her purse. It would have to do for now.

"Yep. Strangest thing though, my uncle is a deputy in town and he said they found a handgun, a knife, and a roll of duct tape in her purse. What average middle-aged woman carries stuff like that?"

A deputy? The urge to curse out loud was strong, but she bit her lip and took a deep breath. As for the weapons found in Lucy's purse, she was astonished they hadn't found more of an arsenal. But then again, he'd said she was only at the grocery store.

A smile crept over her mouth. Lucy would be spitting mad that a grocery store display took her down.

He urged the horse across the street and down through the ditch on the other side. A small gate with nothing keeping it closed other than a simple wrapped chain and trigger snap on the end to connect to a ring on the post was visible in the growing light.

Crime must not be common out here. She considered the double and triple security she lived with back home. Locks, deadbolts, keypads, security guards. Must be nice to rely on snapping a damn gate shut to keep out the wild animals. The bad things in the Hamptons required more than a latch to keep them out.

"No comment?" His soft honey-smooth voice brought her back to the present. His spicy male scent mixed with grass filtered into her nostrils and she inhaled slowly.

"Sounds like Lucy," she answered.

"Is she related to you? I only ask because you also seem to carry an arsenal."

Curious much, wolf-man? She shouldn't share personal information, but something about the warm body and soothing voice won over her need to keep her guard up.

"Not by blood. But she's family. I need to get to the hospital."

Emma tightened her hold on his waist to keep her balance as he leaned to the side to latch the gate. Shoving him out of the saddle crossed her mind at that point, but in all honesty, she wasn't going to get far on her own with nothing more than a gun, her purse, a horse, and no idea which way to the hospital. Going into town and asking around wasn't really an option either.

If Hollis and Grimes were smart—and they were—they would be canvassing the town looking for her, too.

"Quit trying to decide how you're going to ditch me." His voice was steady and even, but his words caught her off guard.

"I'm not."

"Liar. I can hear your heart racing. So either you're planning something or you're terrified. I'm betting on the first, because nothing much seems to scare you."

"Maybe I'm really good at hiding it."

She swallowed and flexed her hands around his stomach again, getting a better grip as the horse climbed another hill.

Shit! Hear my heartbeat? Was it a wolf thing? She'd have to be more careful to steady herself. Meditation would apparently be her friend around these wolf people.

"I would believe that, too. I'm betting you're pretty good at hiding a lot of things. I'm still trying to figure out the stun-gun-carrying-frying-pan-wielding-girl from out of town who knows how to fire an assault rifle."

"You forgot to mention truck-stealing."

"I'm trying to forget that scenario," he said, a

slow chuckle rolling from his chest. "I'm Noah VonBrandt by the way."

She stayed quiet. The last thing she really wanted was for any of them to know who she was. It would only put them directly in Hollis and Grimes's line of fire. They didn't care who or what they had to do to get her back or who they hurt. Though being aligned with one of the wealthiest families in Texas could have its advantages. If the wolf thing was hereditary, there could be a whole other issue that came along with knowing them. *I wonder if those VonBrandt girls that got married in the Hamptons were wolf people, too? Werewolves? I wonder what they call themselves.*

"You might as well tell me. Allan will be able to find your identity sooner than later."

Ah, yes the deputy uncle. She frowned. Later would be fine by her. Unfortunately her picture was plastered all over the news as a missing person. So the likelihood of her identity remaining a secret for very long was next to nil.

"My name is Emma."

"Emma."

The way her name rolled off his tongue warmed her insides, like he was savoring a bite of hot apple pie. There was even the slightest groan of appreciation from deep in his chest. *Damn.* She could not afford to be distracted by a cute guy, much less a cute guy who could turn into a wolf. How did he even exist in a world filled with satellites and cameras on every phone and electronic device?

"No last name?"

"Nope."

"Suit yourself."

They came out of a grove of trees and a huge house sprawled before them. Well, more of a mansion than a house. A large whitewashed barn sat off to the right. Several small corrals and small fields held a variety of horses. The field in front of them had a small herd of cattle grazing over to the left.

A few minutes and a few gates later, they ended up in front of the barn.

Emma slid down from the rump of the horse and stretched uncomfortably as blood started to flow through her ass again. She rubbed it with both her palms and grimaced. It was definitely bruised.

Noah flashed her a smile as he dismounted. "Need any help?"

She glared, yanking her hands away from her bottom. "Did you seriously just offer to rub my ass?"

He shrugged, a twinkle showing in his blue eyes. "I wouldn't be opposed."

"Try it and my trusty stun gun will knock you onto yours again." She patted the leather-fringed purse hanging at her hip. It clanked noisily and she pulled her hand away.

He raised an eyebrow suspiciously, but didn't question the contents of the bulging bag.

Chapter Nine

After cleaning up the horse and stabling him, she followed Noah through the large barn. Rows of stalls lined the center of the building, while several offices and storage rooms lined the far wall down a hallway on the left.

The smell of fresh sawdust and hay was pungently sweet, filling her with a calming peace. She loved spending time in stables. Horses were good company and riding was relaxing after a stressful day of dealing with snarky, rude people who pretended to be all about their charities, when in reality they were merely playing the angles to get more clout.

The horses that stuck their noses out of their stalls to look at them were sleek with coats that shone from hours of meticulous care. The character of a person could be judged by how he cared for his animals. The VonBrandts certainly took pride in their horses and had very good taste. A particularly stunning quarter horse neighed from the last stall they passed on the way to the main door and she couldn't help but stop for a moment to pat his silky muzzle.

"I didn't think you'd have a kind word for another horse after the beating your rump took." Noah crossed his arms over his chest and leaned against the doorframe, waiting.

"It isn't the horse's fault my ass is sore. It's yours," she shot back with a smirk. Even after she'd stunned him and knocked him down, he continued to flirt and tease her. Wolfy Noah was a bit of a glutton for punishment.

"Touché. But I preferred to be in the driver's seat since I was more familiar with the landscape. Plus, I was much less likely to be shoved off and left in the dust."

"True," she answered, sauntering toward him, leaving the quarter horse's stall. "It did cross my mind on more than one occasion."

"I know it did."

"What does your family want with me? Why can't

you let me go to the hospital? It's about the wolf thing, isn't it?" She'd been trying to convince herself it wasn't, but it hadn't worked. A nagging feeling deep in the pit of her stomach said she might be in worse shit with the VonBrandts than she was with Hollis and Grimes.

A telltale sigh slipped from his lips before he answered, and her heart sank to her stomach.

"It does. There are laws about who knows."

"Let me guess," she said, a bitter tone more evident in her voice than she would've preferred. "I'm not allowed to know."

The front door opened and a tall woman with dark auburn hair glared down at her. An unfamiliar sensation clawed its way through Emma's gut --- fear. The cold steel blue eyes of the woman in front of her didn't bode well for her future. She pressed her arm tightly over the handgun holstered to the side of her ribcage. It didn't work though, the woman's gaze narrowed in on the bulge and she pursed her lips into a tight white line.

"No guns," she said, her voice void of emotion. She stretched out her hand, palm up, never letting her gaze drop.

Emma wasn't sure whether to be more frightened or pissed at being ordered to disarm. She hated being vulnerable, but she really couldn't run either. They were out in the middle of nowhere. It was miles into town and she'd have to steal a car or a horse to ever make it there without being caught immediately.

Her eyes flashed up to the corner of the front patio. A small black dome was affixed to the ceiling with a pin-sized red flashing light inside of it. *Strange.* They certainly had state-of-the-art security, for being out in the middle of nowhere. Of course they were protecting more than probably any average person knew or could imagine. Still, digital security meant it would be that much more difficult to slip out if the need arose.

"Gun. Now." The woman spoke again, this time with more force.

"Mom, you don't have to be mean. She's had a rough night."

Mother? This was Noah's mother? Emma studied the woman in front of her again. She could see small similarities in the eyes, but he must take after his father because that's where the likenesses began and ended.

Emma pulled the gun from the holster and placed it gently into Mrs. VonBrandt's hand.

"Is that the only one?"

"Yes," Emma answered without hesitation. She waited for Noah to out the stun gun he knew was in her purse, but he didn't. That small act earned him a few brownie points on the trust scoreboard in her mind. That and his uncanny and continued interest in her after she'd assaulted him three times this evening.

Took a hell of a man to move past something like that and look at her without disdain. He was the only guy she'd ever attacked that had come back for more. Of course he was also the only werewolf she'd ever run across.

It wasn't like she'd had to fend off many advances. Usually her bodyguards' presence at her side shrank the balls on most men who might've had the guts to approach her at all. Being Emma Carrington, daughter of a billionaire arms dealer masquerading as a philanthropist, was a very lonely existence. She could only hope and pray that somehow she could get to Lucy. And that Lucy would be able to get her out of this mess.

There were a lot of *ifs*. A lot more uncertainty than she was used to and the only person who might even be remotely in her court was a wolf-man she'd just met, electrocuted twice, and knocked upside the face with an iron skillet. The odds were certainly *not* in her favor.

They entered the house. Marble tiled floors. Mahogany paneled walls. Persian rugs. Artwork that would've made even her mother a little jealous. It was like walking into one of the Hampton mansions, and it felt a little too much like home— meaning danger probably lurked around every corner in the form of shrewd calculating minds.

A large man entered the room from their left. His broad chest, full shoulders, and darker complexion, not to mention his striking face made him an almost perfect, yet older, replication of the younger man standing by her side. He had to be Noah's father. Though taking into account the stern overbearing attitude, she wouldn't be surprised to hear that he was the deputy sheriff uncle.

"Mom, Dad, this is Emma," Noah started. "Can we talk for a moment first though?"

Noah gently caught her upper arm and pointed toward a room. "Can you wait in there? I need to talk to them first. I'll be right back."

Without waiting for an answer, he ushered her inside the room and slid the large double doors closed behind her.

What the hell? She turned and glared at the two solid oak doors. Dismissed like the help. Her stomach flip-flopped, uncomfortable with being left out of a conversation that potentially had a great deal of importance to the next move in her existence.

"Noah, what the—" the woman spoke more than loud enough to be heard through the doors.

"Mom." Noah protested. "Dad, there are some details you need to know before you make a decision." His voice lowered a few decibels as he continued, but it was still easy to understand.

Emma moved to the door and pressed her ear against the cool glossy wood. The dad growled something unintelligible and the mother hushed him.

"I'm not going to let you steal her life away from her without a fight. She won't either. So get ready." It was Noah again. Sticking up for her, too. *How are they going to steal my life? Kill me?*

That was original.

She rolled her eyes. There's no way he would've brought her to his house just to kill her. He might be some sort of supernatural werewolf, but she'd been in the company of *bad men* before and Noah VonBrandt was not a bad man.

Even as much as her father tried to hide it, she knew he was a killer. It didn't diminish her love for him. He protected and took care of her in the best way he could, but it also lowered her expectations of his role in her life overall.

Killers had a certain spark of humanity missing from their gaze. It wasn't obvious to most, but Emma had learned to pick them out of a crowd. Lucy had taught her what to look for years ago. Flat emotions, coldness, a caustic sense of humor, extroverted, and very intelligent. Only an extremely smart person could kill successfully and not get caught. Most were psychopaths, too.

Not that it helped being able to identify them— she was still surrounded on a daily basis by trained killers. She'd become so desensitized to them, Hollis and Grimes hadn't even been a blip on her radar. Then her parents' friends. If they could be called that. Her father and mother hosted dinner parties with guest lists that would make the everyday Joe piss his pants.

"In the study," a deeper male voice rumbled in response. His father was directing them out of the foyer area and out of earshot.

Damn it.

Chapter Ten

"You can't do this to her," Noah said, leaning against the closed study door. He was slightly conscious of the fact that he was blocking the route to Emma, mostly he didn't trust leaving her in the library for very long on her own. The girl was quick on her feet and didn't waste opportunities.

"The law has been upheld for centuries, Noah. It's there for a reason and was not crafted without great thought to those it would affect."

"She's not just some girl, though. You don't understand. She's got people looking for her already. I'm not sure who Lucinda Craig is to her, but that's where I found her."

"Lucy Craig is in the hospital," Allan said, crossing his foot over his knee and brushing a bit of grass off his pant leg. "She's not going to be much help to the girl from there. Although, I did hear she woke up yesterday."

"Dad, there were men with automatic rifles. We barely slipped out of Craig's house without being spotted. Not sure what they would've done with her, but I'm pretty sure they wouldn't have thought twice about killing me." Noah crossed his arms over his chest and glared straight as his father.

Aaron VonBrandt was a good man. A hard alpha, but fair. He would understand the risks outweighed the advantages of wiping this girl's memory. It could potentially cause the pack more issues in the long run than it might prevent.

"There have to be times where you can bend the rules. I'm not exactly sure who she is yet, but she's not your average girl," he added.

His father shook his head. "There have been no exceptions made in the history of the VonBrandt family. Because of this strict observation of the original laws, we are strong and safe. No one in Somewhere or the surrounding areas suspects us to be anything but human. Our family has thrived and our assets have grown to support the pack well beyond anything we ever dreamed possible. The future generations of our pack have a safe place to run. To live, if they choose, unafraid of being shot or hunted by those who would seek to exterminate all of us."

Noah's chest tightened. He looked to his mother's now weepy eyes and then to Uncle Allan's downcast gaze. Neither would make eye contact with him. It wasn't fair. This girl didn't deserve to lose her identity because he'd needed to take a middle-of-the-night run on all fours.

Damn it.

She'd stunned him twice and nearly knocked him out with a frying pan. Still, he couldn't think of anyone he'd rather be spending his time with. There was something about her. The sheer veracity to live and fight. She wasn't a werewolf, but she had the heart of one. He wanted her. His magick reacted to her as if it were a compass needle and she was due north.

"What if I offered her the bond?" The words slipped out before he could consider them. He didn't want to take them back, though. In fact he felt an even stronger pull toward that solution.

"No," his mother hissed from across the room. "That is not something to be offered to a woman you do not intend to spend your whole life with."

"Luke bonded to Kara before making that

choice."

"Luke had known and been in love with Kara for years, Noah. This is different. You didn't grow up with this girl. She could be a criminal for all you know. You said there were armed men hunting her. What if she ends up dead at the end of this and your one chance to bond is lost for nothing?"

Noah swallowed, his mother's words digesting painfully in his gut. He didn't know Emma at all, but he wanted to. And he didn't think for a moment that she was a criminal, just a girl stuck in the middle of a bad situation. Although, she'd certainly known how to defend herself when attacked. That spoke to some excellent training or growing up around some very bad people.

Still, the bond would prevent his family from hurting Emma without his express consent. It would also make him one hundred percent responsible for her.

He ground his teeth. Bonding with a stranger was probably the stupidest thing he could do, but letting her lose her life and memories wasn't a price he could pay either. He should've been more careful. He should have scouted the area better. It was his fault she'd seen him shift, not hers.

"Noah." His mother's voice was filled with

warning and a slight tremble of fearfulness. "You can't do this. I know you think you should shoulder the blame, but you can't. Bonding with her won't save her. The bond is meant for couples. It deepens a relationship that's already there. It's not meant as a band aid for mistakes. It's meant for marriage. A joining of two souls. It would tear you apart if she left."

A whispered volley of curses came from the other side of the doorway. She was in the hallway, not five feet from the door. The girl didn't know how to follow directions.

He waited to see if Allan or his father had heard her. But both of them were too focused on each other and discussing who would go pick up Siobhan Banfield and her sister Katherine. The two Banfield witches ran the little teashop in town called Books'N'Things. Though they sold a bit more than any of the locals realized —nearly every product in that place was laced with magick.

"Noah, did you hear what I said?" his mother asked, sinking into a red leather captain's chair.

He sighed and nodded his head. He'd heard everything. "I can't let it happen, Mom."

"What if she's married? What if she has a boyfriend already?"

"What if she does, Mom? The family is willing to strip all of that away from her in the blink of an eye. What if it was me in her position? Would you want that for your child?"

"I would if the only other alternative was—"

"Mom." Noah's hands clenched and he resisted the urge to growl. Being disrespectful wasn't going to get him what he wanted. "That's not going to happen," he said, confident that his family wouldn't resort to taking the law into their own hands. Wiping a memory with magick was one thing, but making someone completely disappear was another entirely.

"Noah's right, Tonya," his father interjected. "The pack has never had to resort to that and we won't this time either because the Banfields are going to make sure she doesn't remember a single thing that happened to her since she entered Somewhere this evening."

Emma skulked down the long hallway away from the closed door of the study. Witches? Spells? Amnesia? Who the hell did they think they were?

It's not like she'd ridden some crazy train to an alternate dimension where wizards and witches and werewolves were real. She was in a small honky-tonk Texas town hiding from very real and very crazy assholes with guns who wanted her family's money and arms connections.

And what the hell was this bond Noah and his mother were arguing about? The last thing she needed was to be forced into marrying some crazy wolf-man. That would never work. On that she wholeheartedly agreed with Momma VonBrandt.

Voices carried from down the hallway and Emma ducked inside an open doorway, holding her breath as an unfamiliar man and woman passed by. She counted to sixty before poking her head out. The hallway was clear and the other people were nowhere to be seen.

She continued down the hall and turned through a large dining room, ducking behind a big china cabinet when another woman appeared in the doorway at the opposite end of the room. How many people were in this place and awake before the butt crack of dawn? Were they all wolf people? She banished the terrifying thought from her mind; she couldn't deal with that right now. Right now, she needed to find a damned door out of this mansion and attempt to disappear into the night.

If she could get into town, surely these people would be forced to leave her alone. She knew how it worked. Here she had no leverage. No one knew she was here and no one knew her. If she could get into town, people would see her. She would be missed if these VonBrandts tried to make her disappear.

She waited another minute or two before slipping along the wall of the dining room and into what had to be the kitchen for the place. It was beautiful. She had to credit the VonBrandts for having good taste.

Natural stone covered the floors and parts of the walls. What wasn't stone was beautifully stained wood cabinetry and granite countertops. A massive circular plank table sat to her left with at least ten chairs spaced around it. Wrought iron chandeliers hung from the ceiling in several different places, the lights in the faux candles gave a soft glow to the entire room.

Voices echoed through the kitchen from somewhere, but she couldn't tell where. She knew they would see her in moments if she didn't get her ass out of there. A door lay ahead and to her right behind the table. She made it through and closed it gently behind her as several teenagers filed into the kitchen and surrounded the huge stainless steel refrigerator on the left side of the room.

Emma ducked down and crawled across the small coatroom she'd hidden in. The smell of grass, soil, manure, and sweaty feet filled her nostrils. No wonder they had a room just for their boots.

The outside lay beyond the door on the other side of the room. She threw up a small prayer and pulled the doorknob. The door swung open and she tensed, waiting for the scream of an alarm to sound.

Nothing happened.

She slipped through the opening and shut the door behind her. The growing light of dawn made it easy to see the back of the barn from where she stood. The road out of this place started there. She'd seen several vehicles parked on the other side of the barn's breezeway. If she could hot wire one, maybe she'd have a half-way decent chance of making it into town to the hospital. She had to get to Lucy before Hollis and Grimes did.

Chapter Eleven

The terrain between the stoop and the barn was flat. Short clipped grass and the occasional fence wasn't going to afford much cover. Emma glanced over her shoulder through the two half-French doors and into the kitchen. The group of teens still hovered around the fridge and none of them were facing her direction.

She jumped from the porch step and took off across the yard. The first gate opened with a simple latch, but when she reached the second on the other side of the small corral, it was opened with a push-button keypad. She put a foot up on the middle rail and hoisted herself over and down on the other side. Almost there. The barn would give her cover from anyone looking out the windows of the house.

Making a beeline for the breezeway, she ducked inside a few moments later. The scent of hay and horses filled her lungs and she sighed a small breath of relief.

There had been a truck parked here only a little while ago when she'd been out here with Noah. She hurried down the main aisle and peered out the door at the end —no truck.

Shit.

She couldn't take a horse. Even if it would get her to town faster, the roads weren't a place for them and she wouldn't have anywhere to put the horse once she made it into town. Walking was the only choice.

Hurrying along the main aisle of the barn, Emma exited through the breezeway facing the long driveway. The gravel drive looked like it stretched for miles. It probably did.

She started walking, praying that Noah would keep them talking long enough to give her time to get the hell off his family's ranch. She thought for sure she'd been done for when she let out that litany of curses behind the study door. But the door had stayed shut and the voices plotting the end of life as she knew it had kept on talking. Wolfy bastards.

Noah had one thing right. She certainly wouldn't go down without a fight and they didn't know how accomplished she was at getting her way. They didn't know anything about her yet, but it wouldn't stay that way for long. Someone was bound to turn on the television sooner or later.

The sunrise on her right melted through the shadows across the landscape, making it easy to stay out of the potholes in the road. The fences on either side didn't make her feel closed in until the fields turned to forest. Then, not being able to see around the bends in the road made her nervous. At least with the open fields she could see people coming, but now she was vulnerable. Weak.

She hated feeling weak. Lucy had taught her to always stay on the offensive. Keep your enemies running from you, not the other way around. Right now she was running and it made her sick.

Her hand absently patted the oversized fringed bag and metal clicked against itself. She had a dozen clips for the gun Momma VonBrandt had confiscated, but at least she still had the stun gun. That was something. Plus she knew it worked on werewolf people—at least knocked them on their ass for a few seconds.

The rumble of an approaching engine made her

heart leap in her chest. *No. No. No.* She was still on the VonBrandt property. She hadn't even made it out to Route 16 yet.

Rushing to the fence on her left, she grabbed the top rail and swung one leg over the metal pole. Her other leg followed suit and she slipped to the ground side, backing as carefully as she could into the trees.

Headlights flooded the road where she'd been standing. A black pickup rolled by, moving slower than she'd expected. Both windows were down and she could clearly see a man and woman about her age in the front seats. They were both staring at the tree line.

Emma covered her mouth, sure that the woman in the truck was staring straight at her. The fence, the trees—It was like they didn't matter. How had she known to look for her? She'd been out of the road before they turned the corner.

The woman looked toward the driver and the truck pulled to a stop.

How the hell?

They spoke to each other briefly before the man got out and walked to stand in front of the truck.

"I know you're out there?"

Emma rolled her eyes and cursed under her

breath. He was totally bluffing.

"I can smell you and I can smell Noah's scent on you. You might as well come out. You can't run faster than me." He took a step closer.

"I thought you were wolves, not bloodhounds," Emma hissed under her breath, her heart pounding so hard it was all she could hear in her head. He knew where she was. He was coming closer and closer.

"Luke you're scaring her," the girl in the passenger seat called out, climbing out of the truck.

"Kara, get back in the truck."

"Not a chance," she shot back at him then turned to face Emma once more. "Look, I know you've got to be pretty freaked right now. I was too when I found out. But the VonBrandts are good people. And if Noah is fighting for you, he'll find a way to win."

The male next to her chuckled. "He called me to find you. Come on."

Nope. They were both saying nice things, but Emma knew a trap when she saw one. She took a step backward and a twig snapped under her foot. She cursed and turned to run.

Everything happened so fast. She heard them both yell. Branches whipped her face as she picked her way through the pine trees and brush. Large hands slipped around her waist and yanked her from the ground.

"Let me go!" She fumbled with her bag, trying to get a hand inside it to grab the stun gun. But the clips were in the way and she couldn't find it. "Let me go." She wrenched in his grasp again, but barely twisted a half an inch to one side. "They're going to kill me. Or erase my mind or something horrible. Let me go!"

"No one is going to kill you," he growled in her ear, pulling her hand out of the purse. "But we can't let you wander around town either."

She twisted again and kicked hard.

He grunted and cursed several time, but his grip around her waist never faltered. It was like being locked in a vice. If Noah was as strong as this guy, he'd been holding back earlier.

"I heard them, wolf-boy!"

"Shut up," he snarled. His grip tightened, if that were even possible. "Noah called for help and until he says otherwise, you are coming back to the house.

A ragged groan slipped from Emma's lungs and she sagged, letting her body become dead weight. Fine. If he wanted to lug her to her death, she wasn't going to make it easier on him…or on Noah.

Emma let her body fold nearly in half over his arm. Her hair brushed the ground and the tips of his cowboy boots.

He cursed under his breath and hauled her around to the side of his truck as if she weighed no more than a down pillow.

"Stand up," he ordered, his voice irritated and impatient. He lifted and tried to shove her into the back seat, but kept bumping her head on the side of the bench.

Emma didn't respond.

The woman in the front seat snickered softly, and Emma couldn't help the smile tugging at the corner of her mouth as well. If someone had been watching the scene from the woods, they would've split their sides by now from laughing.

This wolf-man kept trying to push her up into the back seat of the truck and she kept maneuvering enough to make it nearly impossible, unless he caused her an enormous amount of pain.

A soft female voice spoke from the front. "I promise no one wants to kill you. Luke and Noah won't let anything happen."

"Kara, you can't promise that. The pack has rules."

"Killing a girl for seeing one of you turn isn't one of them," she shot back, turning her chair to face them.

Emma straightened in her captor's arms and caught the female's gaze. "Are you a wolf, too?"

The woman he'd called Kara shook her head. "No."

"But you know about them."

"I'm bonded to this one," Kara inclined her head to the man holding Emma. "Are you going to let her go yet, Luke?"

He growled. A scary rumbling animalistic sound came from deep in his chest.

Kara didn't seem scared and that reinforced Emma's confidence that they really didn't mean her bodily harm.

He loosened his left arm from her waist and yanked the purse from her shoulder, handing it to Kara in the front seat.

"I have to get to the hospital. Noah said Lucy is there," Emma said.

"Right now we have to get my brother. Then we can chat about the hospital."

Brother? This was Noah's brother? "Fine." Emma grabbed the plastic handle inside the truck door and pulled herself up onto the bench. When she looked at the man who'd been fighting to get her into the seat, his mouth was hanging open for flies.

He snapped it shut when she smiled. At least she'd gotten into the truck of her own accord and he hadn't been able to shove her in like a sack of potatoes. Dignity wasn't everything, but it was important. These people didn't have the right to push her around just because she'd stumbled onto their secret. She'd kept her fair share of secrets, though this one was a bit different than the average.

"Fine," he growled, slamming the door to shut her in.

"Luke," Kara said, her voice thick with irritation.

Emma could tell they were involved by the way he looked at her with adoration, even though he was peeved. Kara was the same, irritated with her guy's behavior, but still completely devoted to him.

What Emma wouldn't give to have someone like that in her life. But nobody lasted long in the Carrington household. Even the employees came and went like they were on a merry-go-round. The idea that a decent man would put up with everything she had to deal with on a daily basis was laughable.

Chapter Twelve

They pulled to a stop in the driveway in front of the house. Emma started to give Luke a piece of her mind when Noah came barreling out the front door. He yanked open the back door and slid onto the bench next to her.

"Go. Man."

"What about Mom and Dad?"

"Nope, they aren't listening. If crazy old Lucy can help her, she deserves a chance. Gun it, Luke."

The truck jerked and the tires tore through the gravel as Luke swung around and headed down the long driveway.

"What about the whole..." Luke stopped when she caught his gaze in the rearview mirror.

"The wolf thing?"

Noah growled from the seat next to her. "She's not going to say anything. Are you?" The question was directed at her.

"No of course not. I've got enough problems without adding yours to the mix. Get me to Lucy and I'll be out of your hair like I was never here."

"It isn't right, Noah. Mom and Dad know what they're doing. We're going against everything the family has protected for centuries."

"You can dump it on me. I refuse to let her wake up a stranger to herself tomorrow because I didn't scout the area better before I took a late night run. If Dad wants to punish someone, it should be me. I made the careless mistake."

"That's not how it works. Whether you want to take the blame or not. The responsibility to protect the pack rests on Dad."

"Sitting right here," Emma croaked out and leaned against the window, trying to ignore the two arguing men. *The pack? Good grief, how many of them were there?*

"They mean well," Kara whispered over her shoulder to Emma between the seat and the wall of the cab. "They're twins. So they rarely agree on anything."

A half of a chuckle slipped between Emma's lips.

Twin brothers. That certainly explained the need to constantly battle for dominance in the argument.

The truck shot down the driveway and she held onto the seat in front of her as they pulled out onto 16. She was glad they were taking her where she wanted to go. If she could get to the hospital, she could figure it out from there. She needed to see Lucy—hopefully talk to Lucy.

Twenty minutes later they were pulling into the hospital parking lot—St. Bethany Memorial. Luke pulled to a stop in front of the large entrance, and Noah got out first. He opened Emma's door and she hopped out beside him onto the concrete sidewalk, refusing to take his hand.

He raised an eyebrow, but didn't comment.

"Can I have my purse back?" Emma reached toward Kara's open window, but Noah grabbed her outstretched hand.

"Nope, Kara will hang on to that for you," he said, pulling her away from the truck and through the sliding doors of the emergency room entrance.

Jerk. Though she had to give him credit for

remembering what she had in her purse. Of course, he had felt it twice already. Still, if he wasn't giving it to her, he probably didn't intend on letting her go either. Meaning sneaking out of the hospital with Lucy was going to be a little harder than the average walk in the park.

A few people were sitting in the lobby. But it was pretty quiet overall. A group of small couches and single chairs were arranged to one side. A vending machine sat against the far wall and a small coffee bar was open and serving a morning dose of caffeine to all who needed it. The scent of freshly roasted coffee was torture. It'd been too many hours since Emma had downed a cup. The neurons in her brain started to whine, but she shoved down the urge and focused on the task at hand —finding Lucy and getting away from Noah.

She followed Noah to the front desk. A beautiful arrangement of red roses was on the counter to the right and two women in scrubs were speaking to each other in low voices, smiles on both of their faces.

"Excuse me," Noah said, putting a hand on the counter and making eye contact with the younger of the two women. "My friend and I are trying to find out where Lucinda Craig's room is. I know she was brought here after her accident a few days ago."

"I know you aren't related to Lucy. Aren't you one of the VonBrandt boys?" the nurse asked, giving Noah a suspicious eyebrow raise.

Emma moved closer to the desk, bumping her arm into Noah's. Trying to ignore the spark of energy flowing between them, she focused on the nurse who'd spoken.

"She's my aunt. Noah gave me a ride to the hospital."

"Oh, well in that case, I can take you upstairs to her. I'm Shawn Collins," she said, extending her hand. "I was working the ER when she came in and I was also the one who transferred her upstairs. She's probably pretty groggy from the sedatives the docs have her on, but I heard she did wake up from her coma yesterday afternoon."

"You can tell us the room number. I can help her find it." Noah's voice was tense.

Emma knew he didn't want to let her out of his sight, but this was her chance.

"I'll be fine, Noah. Just wait here in the lobby. I want a few minutes alone with Aunt Lucy," she said, patting his arm before she realized she was doing it. She jerked her hand away like she'd touched a hot iron. No touching. She couldn't touch him like that. She refused to be interested in a guy who could turn into an animal. Whose family wanted her dead. *I don't need that drama. Even if it is attached to a heart-stoppingly gorgeous guy who I find myself extremely attracted to.*

Emma's gaze flitted to the pretty blond nurse. "Thank you. I really appreciate the help."

"No problem. This way," she said, grabbing the flower arrangement from the counter.

Emma followed Shawn across the lobby, leaving Noah fuming at the front desk. She hadn't been sure if leaving with the nurse would work, but apparently he was more nervous about making a scene than he was about letting her out of his sight. A quick glance over her shoulder before ducking into the elevator with Shawn gave her a glimpse of an angry Luke storming through the doors with Kara hot on his heels. Her brown-fringed purse was slung over Kara's shoulders along with a pink Vera Bradley cross-body bag. She hated leaving her stun gun and everything behind, but she couldn't afford to come back if she got the chance to slip away.

The doors slid shut behind her and she heaved a sigh of relief.

"She's doing okay." Shawn patted Emma shoulder. "Lucy is a tough old lady."

Emma smiled. "Thank you. It's been a very long night."

"I feel you there. If it weren't for these pretty flowers turning my mood, I'd swear it was a full moon already, but that's not for a day or so I think."

"A full moon?" Emma licked her lips and sucked in a quick breath. She didn't know much about werewolves, but she knew enough from TV and books to know that full moons usually were a problem for them. Unless all of that hype wasn't true.

"Yeah. All the crazies come out on a full moon and march their butts straight into the hospital after crashing their cars or stabbing themselves with butcher knives," Shawn laughed. "Sorry, I remember this one guy last month who swore he saw a wolf with glowing golden eyes out west of town where he was camping in the state park. He was so shook up driving home, he ran right off the road and straight into a tree."

"I didn't think there were any wolves in Texas." Emma fought to keep her voice steady. *Werewolves apparently, though.* She forced her face to remain as emotionless as possible.

"Actually, the VonBrandts own a half dozen

wolf-dog hybrids. They let them run on their ranch land. It doesn't surprise me that one hopped the fence into the state park. But, they've never hurt any person or any livestock in or around town. I've actually seen them in town, riding in the back of Aaron VonBrandt's truck."

"They own wolves as pets?"

"Yeah, I don't know how they control them so well, but they do. No one has ever filed a single complaint as far as I know. Most people in town know about them. This guy just didn't."

"Was the man okay?" Emma asked, pressing a little further. The more she knew about the VonBrandts, the better.

"Yeah, only a little banged up. After we told him he'd either seen a coyote or one of the VonBrandt's over-sized pets, he was fine and more than a little embarrassed. I think he said he was pretty new to town."

Emma sighed. No wonder they were able to hide their secret so well. They'd probably purposefully brought in the hybrids to give the illusion of wolves on the property. *Smart.*

The elevator dinged and the doors opened. Emma followed Shawn out and down a hallway, through a few sets of doors, until she stopped in front of a nurses' station.

"Your aunt is down that hall." She pointed to her right. "Last door on the left, next to the stairwell. I'm glad someone will be with her to help when she goes home in a day or so."

"Thank you," Emma answered. With any luck, she'd have Lucy out of this place and headed out of town before the day was over. She hurried down the hallway, praying to God that Lucy was at least awake enough to sneak out of this place.

Chapter Thirteen

"You let her go up by herself. Noah, what the hell, man?" Luke stomped his way through the lobby toward the chair Noah had sunk into.

Noah glared, warning his brother to stop talking before the outburst made a public scene. It was the very reason he hadn't argued with Emma in front of the two nurses. The last thing their family needed was to be remembered for being the last ones seen with Lucinda Craig's niece—or whatever she was to the woman.

At least Luke took the hint. His brother's mouth snapped shut and he sat on the arm of the chair across from Noah. Kara took up residence in the chair next to Luke and placed her hand on his thigh.

"It's not like she can really go anywhere, Luke.

She doesn't have a car or even her purse." Kara patted the brown bag in her lap with her other hand.

Noah moved quickly, snatching the bag out of Kara's lap and retreating to his seat.

Kara raised an eyebrow and Luke growled low in his chest.

"I'll hold onto this for now."

"What's in it?" Kara asked, curiosity blooming in her bright blue eyes.

"We have to take her to the house, Noah," Luke said, his voice low enough that none of the people milling around the lobby could hear.

"We can't."

"You can't possibly have feelings for this girl in less than twenty-four hours." Luke stood up but didn't move toward Noah. Instead he focused on the television hanging on the wall a dozen feet away.

Noah turned his head and glanced at the screen. Emma's picture popped up along with pictures of a man and woman—Arnold and Ericka Carrington, both found dead on their front lawn. Their throats slit. *Holy shit. Who was this family?* Average people didn't get murdered and dumped on their front lawn.

Noah jumped up, his heart racing in his chest. Emma Carrington. Wealthy. Elite. Mixed up in some bad stuff. No regular person had armed mercenaries tracking them through the night with automatic rifles.

At least it explained why Lucy's closet under the stairs had been stocked like a military locker with weapons and supplies. Genuine fear for Emma's safety wrapped its claws around his chest and squeezed. It didn't make sense that he cared so much about what happened to her. She'd been nothing but a pain-in-the-ass since she'd first lit him up with that damn stun gun.

But he couldn't stop thinking about her. Her curvy but surprisingly strong body. Her soft dark blond hair. Her sparkling blue, intelligent eyes that expertly hid her emotions from the world. Whatever she'd lived through, Lucinda Craig was important to her. He couldn't let this girl suffer at the hands of his family. She'd already lost her parents and probably didn't even know it yet. She couldn't lose her identity too.

His brother pulled out a cell phone and walked toward a row of vending machines.

"What are you doing?" Noah stood, taking a step toward his brother.

"I'm calling dad to tell him where we are. She's not going to come with us easily." Luke's face was grim but serious. He really was going to turn Emma over to their parents without a word.

Not happening. He moved faster than he realized, his hand deep inside Emma's bag, digging for the heavy stun gun in the bottom. Wrapping his fingers around the weapon, he jumped at his brother and pressed the tongs against the skin of Luke's neck.

"Wha—" Luke shuddered and dropped to the floor with a thud.

"Noah!" Kara screamed, falling to the floor next to the chair.

Noah grimaced. He'd forgotten that anything he did to Luke, Kara felt as if it happened to her, too. "Shit, Kara. I'm sorry."

"I'm going t-to b-beat the s-shit out of y-ou, N-noah," his brother growled from the floor where he was still jerking from the electric current the stun gun had shot through his nervous system.

"Not right now." Noah tossed Emma's bag down beside Kara, along with the stun gun, and sprinted across the lobby to the elevator. He had to find Emma before the rest of his family got to the hospital. Luke and Kara would be back to normal in only a few minutes.

"Lucy?" Emma closed the door behind her and turned to the small woman on the hospital bed. A black headband was holding her white blond hair tight to her head. Her skin was paler than she remembered. Lucy was approaching sixty, but she'd always seemed younger and full of energy. Seeing her like this made Emma worry.

An IV fed a line attached to her wrist and an extra-large lump under the covers looked like a leg cast.

"Emma, is that you?" Lucy mumbled, her words slurring. "They've got me on something. I can't move. Damn doctors wouldn't let me go home."

She sounded drunk, but Emma wasn't surprised they'd had to sedate Lucy to keep her in bed, especially if she'd seen a recent newscast. Right now the TV screen was playing some morning news show, but if Lucy had been awake last night, she'd seen the missing persons report on the Carringtons that had been splashed across every channel.

Emma approached the bed and placed her hand on Lucy's forehead, stroking her platinum hair to the side. "I've missed you so much."

"I've missed you, too, sweet girl, but we don't have much time for this right now, do we? Pull the IV out and find my clothes. I know those nurses stuck them in the cabinet over there somewhere. We've got to fly this coop."

Emma smiled. Always telling her what to do. She missed it. Missed feeling the affection that Lucy, even as strict as she was, bathed her in. Just those two words "sweet girl" showed more affection than she'd gotten from her own mother in the past decade.

She carefully removed the IV from Lucy's wrist. Lucy's hand closed around Emma's wrist and Emma felt her heart leap in her chest. Tears welled in her eyes and she leaned over to press a kiss to Lucy's temple.

"It's so good to see you, honey. I love you to the moon and back." Lucy's raspy voice was choked with emotion. She squeezed Emma's wrist tight.

Emma stood and wiped her damp eyes with the back of her hand. "There are people hunting me."

"Help me up," Lucy said, nodding. "I saw blips of the news report last night, that's why they put a damned IV sedative on me. I made the mistake of raving like a lunatic. Have you been to my house yet?"

"Yes, barely got out before my backstabbing asshole bodyguards showed up. If it wasn't for one of the locals, I'd be on foot on your property."

Lucy's eyes sparked to life as she did her best to fight through the sedative clearing her body. "Who's with you?"

"Noah VonBrandt."

"I don't know a Noah, but I know that last name. What the hell was he doing on my property? They own enough land to stay on theirs."

She helped Lucy sit up on the edge of the bed and move to the edge, the cast on Lucy's left leg was going to be challenging. "Is it your ankle?"

"Calf. The damn shelf at the grocery store snapped it. I'm lucky that was the only broken bone, although they said I bruised some ribs too," Lucy said, pulling back the hospital gown and peering down her front. "Sweetheart turn up the volume on the TV. Sportscaster just started and I want to hear what they have to say about the team this season, plus we need to cover our voices. And I damn near missed everything with this stupid head injury. Apparently I've been in a damned coma for a month," Lucy growled.

With a few clicks of the remote, the voices on the

television rose to a clearer level. Emma sat on the foot of the bed, trying not to grin. It was funny, in the midst of any crisis, Lucy always kept track of whatever teams she was rooting for. March Madness had always been a huge part of her life because of Lucy's obsession. She'd forgotten how much she missed it. Without Lucy around, she'd completely stopped watching sports.

"In a shocking upset, the James C. McAdams University Highlanders have won the South Coast Conference title and , for the first time in school history, they will be playing in the NCAA Tournament. Led by sophomore guard and Pac-12-transfer Hamilton Kidd, the Highlanders have pulled out one hell of shocker for the nation. This small, unknown school will now be in the national spotlight, at least while we wait to see what their rank will be in the Tournament. What do you think, Scott?"

"I see a high seed in their future, Ken. Remember, Hamilton Kidd was last year's Pac-12 Player of the Year. That has to factor into the committee's decision."

"We've got to get out of here," Emma reminded her gently, turning toward her beloved guardian. She'd missed her. Missed how life was so much more normal with Lucy around.

"Yes," Lucy said, finally pulling her focus from the television. "The less the VonBrandt boy knows about us, the better. Grab my clothes." Lucy pointed to the cabinet across the room. "It's exciting that our team won though, but I'm pissed I missed the game. That Hamilton Kidd must be a hell of a player."

"Sounds like there will be more games." Emma moved to the cabinet on the wall and opened doors and drawers until she found Lucy's clothes folded neatly in a plastic bag. It was going to be easier said than done, getting away from Noah and his family. She tore the bag open and helped Lucy out of the gown and into her street clothes. If she looked like a discharged patient, the nurses, busy closing out their notes for the night shift, would barely give them a second look. At least that's what she was hoping. The last problem was the stairs. If they took the elevator to the lobby, the VonBrandts would catch them for sure.

"Very true," Lucy murmured.

"Do you think you can make it down stairs with those crutches and the boot on your foot?" She pointed to the tall set leaning against the wall.

"Yes, I'm not that old." She narrowed her gaze at Emma and frowned. "Who's in the lobby?"

"Noah and his brother and the brother's girlfriend. We've got to get out of here, but they won't give me my purse. It's a long story, but we need a place to hide and a car to get us out of town. And we can't go to your house on 16. Do you have another space somewhere in town?" One thing Emma could always count on was Lucy having several back-up plans.

Emma put one of Lucy's shoes on the floor beneath her feet and held it still as Lucy slid her bare foot into it and stood, leaning most of her weight on the bedrail.

"Toss the other shoe back in the cabinet. And yes, always. But we have to go to the farmhouse. My best weapons and the extra passports and paperwork we need are stashed there." Lucy put her hand to her head and sighed.

"We can't. There are people there."

"If they've already looked around, they've left by now. We have to try there first."

"Are you sure you can walk?" Emma handed Lucy the crutches, but stayed close. I'll rest once we swipe a car. Do you still remember how to hot wire one?"

"Let's worry about getting you down three flights of stairs first," Emma said, moving to the door and cracking it enough to peek out. No one was in sight. "We've got to go now, while the nurses are in the middle of shift change. No one will see us if we hurry. Lucky for us, you've got the room at the end of the hall near the stairwell."

Lucy snorted a laugh. "It's not luck. I've been yelling at them, driving them crazy until they moved me to the end of the hall. Hospitals are too noisy for my liking. You know me."

Emma was already nodding her head. A smile spread across her face. "If it's not quiet, you can't hear what's coming." It'd been a while since she'd thought about that mantra.

Lucy swung up behind her on the crutches. "Well?"

"Well what?" Emma said, sticking her head out into the hall a little farther.

"Are we going?"

"Yes, this way." She opened the door for Lucy and watched the hallway for movement while the not-so-slow-cripple made her way to the stairwell door. Even with the drugs still in her system and a broken leg, Lucy wasn't letting it slow her down. Emma was worried it was pure adrenaline though. There was no way Lucy could keep this kind of momentum up for long.

A hum of voices from the nurses' station down the hallway and around the corner kept her pulse racing, but when the elevator dinged, her heart nearly leapt from her chest. One of the nurses spoke up, asking someone why they were here.

Then she heard him. Noah's voice rumbled from down the hall and a shiver ran down her spine to join the butterflies fluttering in her stomach. He did something to her. His presence made her needy and unfocused. It didn't matter what she wanted. She was a survivor and the only way to survive this situation was to get as far away from him as possible.

Emma closed the stairwell door behind her and prayed they could make it down the stairs and out of the building before wolf-boy sniffed them out.

She rushed down the stairs behind Lucy, pausing every few steps to listen for the door opening.

"What's got your panties in a wad, Emma?"

"I heard him. Just before we went through the door. And my panties are not in a wad. Thank you very much."

"Sure seems like he's got you a little edgy."

Emma ignored the last comment and continued down the stairs. They reached the bottom floor and exited the stairwell into a main hallway of the hospital.

Lucy pointed to her left. "We can go out this way."

"It doesn't lead back to the main lobby?"

"Nope. Don't worry, sweetie. Unless that VonBrandt boy can follow a trail like a bloodhound, he'll be shit out of luck when he gets to the bottom of those stairs."

Emma gulped. She hadn't even considered the fact that he might be able to sniff her out like a dog following a scent. *Shit.*

"Let's get out of here before someone recognizes you."

Banishing the momentary flash of panic, Emma followed Lucy down the corridor, smiling at the random employees who passed them. No one paid them any notice. Apparently shift change was the perfect time to break someone out of a hospital. Everyone was more worried about signing themselves off the clock to care if a crippled older woman and a stranger slipped out the back entrance.

Chapter Fourteen

"Lucy, I think they are still at your house," Emma said, pulling over into the grass and turning off the headlights of the old 1980's Dodge they'd swiped from the hospital parking lot. Hopefully, whatever old geezer owned it wouldn't have a stroke when he found it was missing.

"Lucy?" Emma pulled the shifter into park and looked over at the woman she called aunt—the woman who in reality she considered her mother.

Lucy didn't respond. Her head lolled a little to one side, but Emma could hear her steady breathing. She was a tough broad, but getting down those stairs, out of the hospital, and out to the back of the parking lot where this old hunk of steel had been parked was quite the journey for someone who'd been in a coma up until yesterday afternoon. She'd known the burst of energy would only last so long.

The sun was fully visible now and in a few minutes, the last bit of dawn would fade and the bright orange truck was going to stick out like a sore thumb if anyone took a look out the window of the house.

Emma threw the truck into reverse and slowly started backing up the way she'd come. If she could get around the curve in the driveway, behind a bank of trees, the truck would be hidden from view of the house. But where after that? She didn't know anyone in town and Lucy needed somewhere to rest.

She took a deep breath. *One problem at a time, Emma. One problem at a time.* Right now she needed to get out of sight of the house. Carefully, she maneuvered the truck backward and around the bend. A sharp rapping on the glass of her window elicited a girl-about-to-die-in-a-horror-flick scream that she was ashamed to hear come from her throat. Her heart stopped in her chest for at least a whole five seconds and air refused to be drawn into her lungs.

Noah stared at her through the glass. *Deja vu*

much? At least this time he wasn't naked. Once she managed to swallow her heart back down into her chest and draw a breath, she wound the window crank on the door and lowered the glass.

"I know, I know. This is where you Taser me. But seriously, you need my help. Lucy looks like she needs some rest and I don't think your ex-military friends in the farmhouse would be keen on keeping her alive."

Emma took a deep breath and narrowed her gaze at Noah. "How the hell did you find me so quickly? And it's not a Taser. It's a stun gun. But, seriously, how did you find me? There were no cars following me out of town. I made sure."

"I wasn't in a car. I was running."

Emma's mouth opened, but words wouldn't form. "I. You. Wha-a—"

"Look, we need to find a place to crash while we figure out what to do. If not, you won't have a choice because I guarantee my family is only a few minutes behind me."

"Fine!" Emma slapped the steering wheel with both palms. "Where do you suggest we go?"

"There's a big empty house for sale on Jericho Lane. Been empty for a month. The Thompsons had to move. No one will think to look for us there," Lucy said taking a deep breath.

"Lucy!" Emma breathed a sigh of relief. But Lucy wasn't looking at her; she was talking to Noah.

"Do you know it?" Lucy asked.

Noah nodded. "Scoot over. I'm driving." He yanked open the door and Emma moved to the middle of the bench. Before she could catch a breath, they were on 16 and barreling toward town.

She wanted to ask where they were going. She wanted to ask a lot more than that, but for now she would hold Lucy's clammy hand and wait. For now he was protecting her from his family and her would-be-kidnappers-possibly-murderers. For now she would go along with it.

As tough as Lucy was, Emma knew she needed to be in a bed, at least for a while.

Noah drove carefully through the old part of town and headed west into a small development where the houses sat on half-acre and acre lots. He didn't think Lucinda Craig knew anyone in town, yet somehow she'd known the old Thompson couple had left their house last week and moved out of state ahead of schedule. Movers weren't supposed to arrive to pack the house for another week or two. It would be perfect as long as there wasn't an alarm system on the house.

His main concern right now was to get Mr. Henry's blasted orange pickup truck off the roads before someone saw him driving it. Out of every vehicle in the hospital parking lot, they had to take this one. Luckily it was morning rush and everyone was more concerned about getting to work than paying attention to a college kid driving this familiar orange classic instead of its grumpy old owner.

The second thing on his mind was how his leg and Emma's kept brushing against each other. He'd already caught and held back his hand several times from lowering to her leg and stroking it. He knew better. She probably had another Taser hidden somewhere on her person, just waiting to send him convulsing to the floor again.

Her scent invaded his space and he did his best to banish thoughts of tasting her skin, her lips, and anything else she might let him get close to. His jeans fit uncomfortably tight and he bit back a groan, hoping she wouldn't notice.

They finally turned down the street where the Thompsons lived. He pulled into their driveway and parked behind the house on the grass out of sight of the road.

"There's an alarm system warning sticker on that back window." He leaned against the steering wheel, exhaling a long sigh.

"I can get us in," Lucy said softly. "Help me get out of this truck."

Really? Noah looked across Emma to the older woman leaning against the seat. "How?"

"I know the code."

Emma's face took on an incredulous look as well.

"Y'all quit looking at me like I've lost my mind. Mrs. Thompson and I went to the gun range together twice a week. I watched their dogs every time they were out of town."

Noah grinned. "Alright, then." Mystery solved.

Minutes later they were standing in the Thompsons' kitchen. The alarm was off and reset. Noah locked the door behind them and turned to see Emma and Lucy disappear down the hallway into a bedroom.

He went to the large brown leather couch and sank into the soft pillowy cushions. It'd been a long night. One in which no one had gotten any sleep. He was horny, cranky, and worried about how long it would take for his family to track him to this house. If not his family, who and what was coming after Emma?

Emma walked through the living room and into the kitchen without a word. He watched through slitted eyes as she fixed a glass of water and dug around in the cabinets until she produced a loaf of bread.

The scent of yeast made his stomach do a flip. He was hungrier than he thought. Swinging his legs to the side, he pushed himself up off the couch and joined Emma in the kitchen.

"Is there enough to share?"

"There's plenty," she answered, taking four pieces from the plastic bag and then sliding it across the counter toward him.

She pulled three plates from the cabinet above the sink, pushing one toward him. "There's not a lot in the fridge, but I found butter and strawberry jam."

"I'm not picky, just hungry."

She chuckled, slathering the bread she'd pulled out with a layer of butter and then a layer of jam. "I'll be right back. I need to give this to Lucy," she said, grabbing a plate from the counter and leaving the kitchen.

He buttered his slices while she was gone and

took a seat at the small antique kitchen table.

Emma reappeared from the bedroom and took her plate from the counter. She slid into the chair opposite him and then hopped up again without taking a bite.

"Do you want some water?"

"Yes, thanks." It was a mistake, but he couldn't help glance at her ass as she walked away. "Why are you being nice to me?"

"Because you helped us." She set a glass of ice water in front of him and sat in the chair opposite him.

"What's going on with you?"

"Whatever do you mean," she said, a smirk curving the corners of her mouth into the cutest smile. It made him want to kiss her even more. Her blond hair dropped in front of her face and he leaned over, brushing it from her cheek before he could stop himself.

Her heartbeat sped, making the vein in her neck pulse faster, and a slightest gasp of air rushed from her lungs. His fingers lingered, grazing over the lobe of her ear before he sank into his seat and dropped his hand to the table. Her eyes widened and he caught sight of the same heat he felt beneath his skin mirrored in her azure gaze. He bit back a groan when her tongue slipped between her lips and wet them.

"My dad associated with people of the unsavory sort." Her eyes dropped to the tabletop and her shoulders slumped forward. "It cost him."

"Do you know…"

"That they're dead?" She glanced at him and picked up her toast, taking a big bite. "No, I hadn't heard an updated newscast that announced it, but I knew." She swallowed the bite she'd taken and took a slow sip of water. "What did the news say?"

"They were—"

"It's okay. You don't have to say. I know it's going to be bad."

"I'm so sorry. They were found on their front lawn this morning. It didn't give specifics, but, Emma…are they trying to kill you, too?"

"Not right off the bat. They want my family's money first, I'm sure."

"Is Lucy really your aunt?" He asked robotically, shocked that she was showing no emotion whatsoever over the death of her parents.

Emma shook her head. "She was my guardian until I was sixteen years old. I call her my aunt because it was the closest family name I could use without calling her mom. She raised me. I saw my real mother a few times a year growing up, usually at holidays."

"So…"

"I'm fine. I'll be fine. I just need Lucy to get back to normal and then we can leave. You'll never have to see me again or worry about your secret. I won't tell anyone."

That wasn't what truly worried him. She was the one he'd been waiting for. Since meeting her, every thought he had centered on her and his magick hadn't stopped vibrating every time they touched.

"My family won't accept that. They will hunt you."

"Then they can get in line," she spat back. "I've lived through three kidnappings and a half dozen attempted murders. They finally got my parents. Now I have no reason to stay I can disappear with Lucy."

Disappear? The thought of never seeing Emma again felt like someone was strangling him with barb wire. He wanted to know everything about her. He wanted to protect her from whatever it was that had chased her over the course of her entire life. No one should feel so hunted that their only recourse is to drop off the grid.

"Where would you go?"

She smiled. "An island somewhere. It will be nice to finally be able to relax. I need you to keep your family away long enough so that we can slip out of town."

"Our laws won't allow you to leave, knowing what you do about our family."

"Your laws. You have wolf laws?"

He nodded and swallowed the last piece of his toast. "We have another problem, too."

"The full moon tonight?"

His mouth dropped open for a second before he snapped it back shut. "How did you—"

"The nurse said something about the full moon rising today or tomorrow. She couldn't remember. But it's tonight, isn't it?"

"Yes."

"What happens to you? Will you be dangerous?" He heard her pulse speed up again, but she took several long breaths, evening it out quicker than he expected. In fact she was taking this whole man-to-wolf transformation stuff better than anyone he'd ever seen.

"I won't be dangerous unless I want to be. The full moon traps me in wolf form until the sun rises again."

"But that means your family will be changed, too,

right?"

"Most," he answered. "My mother isn't a werewolf. And she's pretty convinced that you can't be trusted."

"They don't know me."

"We don't trust anyone, Emma. It's not like we are making an example out of you. No one is allowed to see what you saw unless they join the family." He shifted in his seat and took a quick sip of water. His clammy hands left a print on the glass and he traced his initials in the remaining condensation. The heaviness in his heart grew, tightening his chest until it was painful to breath. He couldn't stand the thought of his mother demanding Emma's memories be wiped.

"I won't let them hurt you."

"How can you stand against your entire family? Even your brother was ready to throw me to the wolves, pun intended." Emma tapped her manicured nails against the top of the table. Each *tap tap tap tap* made his skin itch. His mother's words of warning rolled around in his head, but everything inside him wanted to mark her and claim her as his and be done with this entire mess with his family. That would only leave one problem—the mercenaries chasing her.

Chapter Fifteen

"What kind of bond were you arguing about with your mother?"

Noah took the freshly washed dish from her, dried it, and placed it in the cabinet. "It's a spell that would bind us together permanently. If we bonded, my family would have no choice but to accept you. It's complicated. Aren't you freaked out enough?"

"A magic spell…you're just full of surprises. And yes, the wolf thing has me unsettled for sure, but if you'd seen half the things I have, knowing they were committed by a human and not a wild predator, you wouldn't be as surprised by my lack of freak-out." She handed him the last plate and pulled the stopper in the sink full of sudsy water. "What I can't believe is that you've kept this a secret for so long in a world full of cell phones and satellites."

"My dad's hybrids help with our cover here in town."

"The dogs?"

"Wolf-dog mixes. He makes a point to take a couple of them into town from time to time. People see them. Then the howling and occasional sightings are easily played off. Our ranch butts up against the state park, so we have miles and miles of protected land where no one is allowed to hunt." He dried his hands and gestured to the living room. "How is your aunt doing?"

"She's fine. Still a little woozy and tired from everything. I told her she didn't need to get up. At least for now, she's listening to me."

A spark seared his arm when he came in contact with a sliver of flesh on the small of her back. She must've felt it too, because she hurried forward, breaking their contact. Disappointment flooded his body at the rejection… or was it fear. He'd seen her desire for him in the truck. Feelings like that couldn't be mistaken for something else. But she could be scared. Just because she said she wasn't didn't mean she wouldn't lie to make him feel better.

She'd straight up said she was being nice because he'd helped them. Maybe that was the only reason. Maybe as soon as she got what she wanted, he'd just be the wolf-man again and she'd be brandishing another cast-iron skillet. Life didn't usually follow the path of a fairytale.

Didn't mean he couldn't try to push it in that direction, though. He was a werewolf after all. Magick was in his blood.

Emma couldn't shake the attraction she felt. The touch at the table when he'd brushed back her hair. Then again when he'd touched her back as they'd left the kitchen. She was attracted and horny. And he was cute. A werewolf nonetheless, but still damned hot. She shouldn't be thinking about him. That was the last thing she needed clouding her judgement. But every time she looked at him, breathed in the spicy scent of his aftershave, her legs went to jelly and her panties dampened. Then there was the memory of his sleek hard body in the moonlight just before she stole his truck and electrocuted him.

Problem. Major problem. His family wanted to erase her memories and Hollis and Grimes wanted to steal her father's wealth and connections. And Noah…Noah seemed like he wanted something completely different. He wanted her. Only her. Not Emma Carrington, daughter of a billionaire crime family, but Emma Carrington, a girl who'd been starved for affection since her father removed the only human on earth from her life who had ever loved her—Lucy.

Emma craved the way Noah looked at her. The way his eyes followed her through the room as if he'd never get tired of staring. Then there was his touch. Electrifying. That was the best description she could come up with. It was like every nerve in her body fired when he touched her. She wanted more. She wanted much more.

The question now was…would he give it to her?

She sat down on the center cushion of the couch and held in a sigh of relief when he took the cushion on her right. The foam of the seats sank and their legs touched, sending that same spark of desire coursing through her body. She licked her lips, trying to decide whether or not to kiss him now or wait and see what he did.

Fate didn't let her contemplate long. One of his

hands cupped her face and slid to the back of her skull, cradling her head ever so gently as he covered her mouth with his. His other hand slid around her waist and tugged her body closer to his.

Her fingertips slid up his taut arms toward his neck and she threaded her fingers through his wavy hair. She pulled him closer, opening her mouth, inviting him to take more. The invitation was not ignored. His tongue swept through her mouth, tangling with hers in a battle of desire. Both of them gasped for air as Noah pulled her into his lap as he laid back against the arm of the couch.

One of her knees slipped between his legs, making her hip rub against his very stiff erection.

He groaned into her mouth, nipping at her lip with his teeth. Then his hand moved to her ass and pulled her higher up onto his chest, grinding her throbbing sex against his, her lycra yoga pants not affording much of a barrier against his jeans. She could feel him as though she were naked and wished she was.

His mouth trailed from her mouth, down the side of her neck, feathering her skin with light kisses and nips. He tugged her shirt off her shoulder and kissed his way down onto her collarbone.

Emma let her hands explore the contours of his

body, slipping her fingertips beneath the hem of his shirt and tracing the lines of his sculpted ab muscles. She'd wanted to touch him there since seeing him last night. If she was being really honest, she'd wanted to touch every part of him since last night.

"How far do you want this to go?" he asked, between breaths.

She could feel his heart pounding against her chest, nearly in time with hers.

"Is it going to do something to me?"

He chuckled as he pressed his lips to her shoulder again. "I sure hope so…but not in the way you're thinking."

A giggle slipped from between her lips as his comment registered. "I want as much as you will give me." The words spilled from her lips before she could think them through, but they were still the truth. She couldn't deny the attraction she felt.

He pulled her mouth against his again and claimed it with an animalistic growl that made her body tremble with excitement. He stripped off her shirt a second later and massaged her breasts through the thin lace of her bra. His fingers worked her nipples until they stood at attention, pressing against the constricting lace.

She moaned into his mouth and slid her palms along the lines of his sculpted chest, then down until she felt that deep indentation near his hip that led below the waist of his pants—that "v" that drew a woman's eye like a moth to a flame.

"Your shirt needs to come off," she said, pulling away from his mouth for a moment.

He complied and they were quickly skin to skin. *Absolute perfection.*

A quick motion unhooked her bra. She arched her back, lifting high enough for Noah to pull it free from her breasts and toss it to the floor. His hands closed around her waist, dragging her higher onto his chest until his mouth was even with her swaying breasts.

When his lips closed around one of her nipples, she gasped for air. He sucked and licked and pulled, holding her against him with one arm and slipping his other hand between them. His fingers trailed down her stomach, tickling until he reached the hem of the yoga pants she was wearing. He didn't stop there. His fingers continued their downward descent until they slipped between the wet lips of her sex and found the object of their desire—her swollen clit.

She jerked against his hold, a wordless scream on

her lips as an orgasm rushed through her, exploding like a thousand firecrackers all at once. It took everything she had not to make the walls of the Thompsons' living room shake. Lucy was down the hall and she didn't need her barreling out of the bedroom, waving her crutches, thinking something terrible had happened only to find them both naked from the waist up and Noah's hand down her pants.

He moved his hand, giving her throbbing sex a short reprieve from the exquisite torture his fingers had brought. She panted for breath and buried her face in the pillow above his head while his mouth hungrily continued to sample her breasts.

A moment later, Noah grabbed her ass and stood with her still half wrapped around him.

"How?" she gasped, wrapping her legs around his waist and locking her ankles together. There shouldn't have been any way he could've lifted her and his body the way he did.

"There are perks to having a little magick in the blood."

"Show-off."

He smiled that adorable kiss-me-I'm-so-cute grin and Emma couldn't resist.

She planted her lips against his again as he walked with her down the hallway, careful to keep her knees from bumping against the walls.

"Which room?"

"The last one. Lucy is in the first one," Emma whispered into his ear, nipping at his earlobe and relishing the shiver that skittered through his entire body. Big, strong, wolf-man could be brought to his knees with a touch of her teeth.

He groaned, twisting his ear free of her mouth as he entered the last bedroom at the end of the hall. As soon as the door shut behind them, he put her down and stripped her of her yoga pants in one swift tug. She stepped out of them and stood quietly, tense and waiting for him to make the next move. She was naked. Exposed. Feeling more vulnerable than she'd ever felt with a guy before.

Why did he affect her so strongly? Why did she dread the idea that she might not see him again after all this ended, after she and Lucy disappeared?

"Don't be sad, beautiful. I told you I won't let anyone hurt you," he said, his voice barely louder than a murmur. He stepped closer and caressed her face with his knuckles. "I want you more than anything I've ever wanted in my life."

A single tear rolled down her cheek. Her heart broke, knowing she wouldn't get to stay. She was a realist. Her parents, Lucy, her bodyguards, none of them had allowed her to grow up to be anything else.

Noah thought he lived with the stress of his secret hanging over his head, but it was nothing compared to the life she'd lived. To the life she had to run from. People didn't try to kill Noah VonBrandt. But if she stayed… they might.

Right now. In this moment. She wanted a small taste of what she knew she'd have to give up. She wanted him more than anything, too.

Emma let her mouth turn up into a smile. "I want you, too. So much it hurts."

Chapter Sixteen

They moved to the bed and Emma lay on the soft quilted comforter. Her pulse raced and every nerve ending in her body was attuned and anticipating his touch. Noah was everything she wanted in a man. Intuitive, stubbornly protective, gentle, yet strong enough to handle her baggage without freaking out. The werewolf bit was still going to take some getting used to, but so far she hadn't seen many downsides to the supernatural heritage he claimed—except that his family wanted to perform magickal brain surgery on her. That was a bit of an issue.

Noah's lips twitched. "I want to taste you."

"Isn't that what you've been doing? All I have to do is close my eyes and I can still feel your lips on my skin." She took a deep breath and scooted to the middle of the bed.

He followed, his movements predatory and smooth as he climbed onto the mattress from the foot and wrapped his arms around her thighs. A gentle tug slid her down the length of the large bed and he settled himself on the floor on his knees, his face eye level with her sex. His warm breath on her bare flesh made her womb clench and sparks cascade throughout her body. Tension coiled in her stomach. It wouldn't take much to make her implode into the dimension of ethereal space known as the female orgasm.

"Close your eyes and you will feel it again," he said, his deep voice rumbling against her thigh.

A needy gasp slipped between her lips, but she pressed her eyelids tight and shivered, waiting for the first touch.

He lapped at her slit, and a sexy-as-hell moan sent vibrations through her core as his well-defined arms tightened around her hips, preventing her from escaping his tongue for even a second.

"You taste like honey, Emma. I'm going to make you come so hard, you'll be hanging on to that comforter for dear life. Then I'm going to do it again."

She gulped, mentally making her fingers release the wads of bedding she'd already bunched up.

His tongue delved into her sex and then pulled out, swirling instead around her throbbing clit. A moan rumbled in her throat, but she swallowed it. Noise wasn't an option. Lucy was down the hall, but Noah wasn't going to make it easy.

Good God. She needed a little more and she'd be sailing.

His fingers slid inside her and his mouth closed around her clit, pulling hard.

Her breath choked in her lungs as her nerve endings fired. The tightness that had been coiled in her belly contracted even tighter and then sent her spiraling into blissful abandon. She pressed her lips tightly together, willing the primal shout building inside to stay inside.

She shuddered through the last wave of her orgasm while Noah rose to his feet, standing between her legs. He'd shed his pants and already pulled a condom onto his cock. Her insides clenched in anticipation, ready and waiting for his hard length to be buried within.

"You are so beautiful," he said, leaning forward, slipping an arm beneath her ribcage, lifting and pulling her toward the top of the bed as he crawled over her.

She pushed with her feet, helping to propel herself faster up the length of the bed.

He settled his body over hers, his hard muscles fitting against her curves perfectly. She raised her legs, sliding them up his and then wrapped them around his waist, lifting her core closer to his waiting erection.

To her surprise, he grabbed her legs and pushed her thighs forward until they nearly touched her breasts. Then slid inside, slowly and purposefully, filling her completely.

Her heart skipped a beat and she gasped, taking him all in at once. It'd been so long. She was so tight.

God, he felt so good.

"Is this what you wanted, Emma?"

She nodded her head, keeping her lips tightly pressed together, trying to contain the whimpers of pleasure fighting duplicitously against her will to escape.

He drew out her pleasure, completely in tune with her body. His hands played with her breasts, stroking and kneading them until they ached for his mouth. He sped up his thrusts when she could take it and backed off when she felt the overwhelming urge to come apart.

She felt boneless beneath him. Her extremities trembled with the need for release, but he kept it just out of reach. Desire raged inside her and she wanted the second climax he'd promised.

"Please," she begged, her breathing ragged. Sweat coated her skin from head to foot and strands of her long blond hair were pasted to her forehead and shoulders.

He complied, dropping her legs to his sides and settling into the cradle of her hips. His mouth closed around a peaked nipple. One of his hands slid upward, slipping behind the base of her head while the other ventured south, finding its mark between their slick bodies.

One last thrust and the light brush of his calloused fingers over her already stimulated clit was all it took. It was as if every muscle and nerve ending fired at the same time. Emma arched off the bed, burying her face in the crook where his neck met his shoulder, muffling her scream as she soared into bliss.

His body jerked and stiffened against hers as he chased her pleasure with his release. He muffled the growl that shook his entire body against the curve of her neck.

A shiver ran through her and the tension in his body fled, quickly replaced by a tenderness Emma had never before experienced. . His mouth trailed along her slick skin, pressing kisses against her breasts, her neck, her chin, and then her mouth. He seemed to be in no hurry to flee the bed and leave her wondering if he'd enjoyed it or was satisfied.

"You. Were. Amazing," he said, punctuating each word with a kiss to her lips.

"Thank you," Emma answered as another blast of heat warmed her cheeks.

"I love that you are still blushing after everything we did. I have a feeling getting to know the real Emma Carrington is going to be a full-time gig. Though one I'm going to thoroughly enjoy."

The cutest grin split his face and his blue eyes sparkled with interest. And not just an interest in her naked body or how much money her family controlled, he was genuinely interested in her. Hell, he was protecting her from his family, going expressly against rules that they had been following for who knew how long. He thought he had time to get to know her, but she knew it was an illusion. The second Lucy was back to herself, they would slip away into the ether and she'd never see Noah VonBrandt again. Her heart constricted and she struggled to drag in a breath at the thought.

In less than twenty-four hours, this guy had managed to crack the tough shell she always kept around her heart. She couldn't fall for him. It couldn't happen.

"There are things about me that you don't want to know. We should enjoy the time that we have. Nothing is guaranteed in life."

He rolled to her side and pulled her with him, nibbling at her shoulder. "Why does that sound like a goodbye?"

"I can't stay in Somewhere, Noah. There are people hunting me. When the drugs finally clear Lucy's system today, she will be ready to leave."

"I already told you I won't let anyone hurt you. Not my family and not those assholes at Lucy's house." He snarled out a growl and Emma gasped, watching his eyes flash gold for a few seconds.

"It's not that simple. Those assholes will kill people to get to me. I can't put you or anyone else in danger. Their partners already brutally killed my parents. You don't know how ugly this could get."

Noah released her and rolled from the bed in silence. He disappeared into the adjoining bathroom for a few moments. He returned cleaned up, but still naked with a washcloth in his hand.

She stayed silent as he tenderly bathed her thighs and girly-parts with the warm washcloth. The care he was showing was so different from anything she'd experience with any guy before. Usually sex was just sex. After which, each party cleaned up and went about their day, but Noah caressed her body as he rubbed, dragging the tips of his fingers across her skin until her heart began to pound with renewed arousal.

How did he do that? How did he make her completely forget that she needed to slam down the walls around her heart? Instead he opened them wide, showing her how much sunlight she'd been missing for so many years.

The day stretched out, long and tense. She and Noah barely spoke and her heart broke for what she knew she was losing. Lucy started to come out of her fog around noon, but Noah spent most of the day standing or sitting by the front window, staring out at the street. No one should be able to track them. The old truck didn't have GPS and neither of them had phones. He'd told her he dumped his at

Lucy's house when he found them in the driveway. Still he watched.

Chapter Seventeen

Noah took a deep breath, forcing himself to ignore the pain in his chest. She might still be leaving town in a few hours, but he had a decision to make. A decision he'd been struggling with for the entire day. Either he marked her now, before the sun set and the full moon rose and his family was able to track him by scent, or she would be hunted by more than just mercenaries.

His family wasn't evil, but they wouldn't leave her alone. Not if they believed she represented a threat to the family—to the pack. Her knowledge of their secret was enough. Not only would she have to worry about mercenaries, she would have supernatural hunters looking for her every day for the rest of her life. She would never be able to stop running…if she could manage to stay ahead of the wolves at all.

But, if he bonded with her, everything his mother had said was true. He would lose the chance to bond with someone else and he and Emma would forever be linked. Could he live with that? If she had to leave because of the men who killed her parents, would he be able to let her go?

With the bond, she would be protected from his family and from most injuries. She would be his, but not completely. His heart would ache for her and a hole would form in his soul that no other woman could ever fill. His mother's words weren't idle warnings. Magick wasn't something to be toyed with. There was always a price.

Light footfalls behind him brought him back to reality. Emma's light citrusy shampoo scent filled his lungs. He wanted nothing more than to bury his face in her blond silky tresses again.

"We are almost ready to go. Thank you for your help. I know going against your family was hard. We will be gone soon. Lucy is taking a quick shower before we go…Will they forgive you?"

"I have to leave you in a few minutes," Noah said, the words sticking in his throat like a stale hunk of bread.

"Because it's nearly sunset?" Emma asked, stopping a few feet short of his chair. "Are you okay?"

"They will forgive me, but they won't forget you. They will hunt you to the farthest corners of the world. I need to bond with you in a way that will protect you from my family permanently."

"What are you talking about? I can't stay with you, Noah. I already said I had to leave." He saw tears welling in her widening eyes.

"If they catch those men, you could come back, though."

"Maybe. But I heard your mother. She said your bond was a one-time thing. I can't even stay with you. It's not right," she said, stepping closer, cupping his cheek in one of her hands.

He settled his hand over hers and then pulled it to his mouth, tasting her sweet skin with his lips. "Like I told my mother, it is my choice. And I would give it to you. If I don't, I'm sentencing you to a life of being hunted by my family. I won't let them steal the only thing you have left. I can't imagine losing my parents, but losing my self would be worse."

"How can they take my memories? How is it even possible?"

"Magick can do things you can't imagine."

"Like turn a man into a wolf?"

He nodded. "Like turn a man into a wolf."

"It's not fair to you, Noah. She said it was for the woman you will marry."

The light from outside was waning and the sun had almost reached the horizon. "Please, Emma. Let me do this. Maybe one day you can be that woman."

A single tear rolled down her cheek and he stood, pulling her tight to his chest. She fit so perfectly, her curves complementing the hard edges of his body.

"You have to tell me it's what you want," he said, his voice choked with emotion. "Please."

She nodded against his chest and then pulled away from his embrace. "Yes," she murmured.

He sighed, relief flowing through him like someone had opened a dam high in the mountains and now the water was rushing forward like a raging animal freed from its cage. But it was too late.

"Emma, I—" The first spark of the change came on before he could finish his sentence.

Emma's chest tightened. Noah growled and then pushed her away. Something shimmered in the air around his body and he shifted right before her eyes, struggling and squirming on the floor until the human clothing fell off of his animal body.

Holy shit. That just happened.

Again.

Dark brown and gray fur covered him from his black nose to his bushy tail. His eyes glowed gold for a moment before turning whiskey brown. He cocked his head and a long whine rumbled from his throat.

"Now what?"

He gave her a low *wuff* as she gathered up his clothes and stuffed them under a seat cushion so Lucy wouldn't see. She expected the bedroom door to open any minute.

And it did.

"Emma, are you ready?" Lucy asked, making her way out into the living room faster than anyone should've been able to move on crutches. "Fuck! What is a wolf doing in the living room?"

"It's Noah's dog. He left him to watch over me. He had to go deal with a family emergency."

The wolf—Noah—cocked his head to the side

again and sat on his haunches, moving his gaze back and forth from Emma to Lucy.

"Hmmm, I forgot the VonBrandt's kept hybrids as pets. Still, up close, he really looks more like a wolf than a dog. Did Noah take the truck? We need that to get to my farm."

"What about the guys camped out there waiting for us to come back?" Emma perched her hand on one hip and tried to keep her focus on Lucy, but her gaze continued to shift to Noah.

"We need to stop at one of my stashes for supplies on the other side of town. I'm going to take care of those assholes, no worries. We'll tie them up and drop them on the sheriff's doorstep on our way out of town."

"I lost my purse. I don't have an ID or anything."

"Don't worry, sweetheart, I have aliases for both of us. You can't get out of the country using your real name anyway. They will be watching for it on flight manifests." Lucy swung herself closer to the front door. "The wolf will have to stay at the farm. Hopefully he can find his way home from there."

Emma's lips twitched. "I'm sure he'll be fine."

Her aunt snorted. "He'd better. We don't have time to babysit a dog. Didn't you tell him we had to leave?"

"He knew. He only wanted me to be safe."

Lucy pulled open the door. "Go wait by the truck. I'm going to set the Thompsons' alarm."

Emma patted her leg without thinking, urging the big wolf-dog to follow her out the door. She wasn't at all surprised when he rubbed up against her leg as they exited the house. He stayed glued to her side every step of the way from the door to the truck, his big paws padding silently on the green lawn.

"I'm sorry we ran out of time, Noah," she whispered, running her hand along the soft fur of his head and down his neck.

A mournful whine came from his throat and he pressed himself even closer to her legs.

"I'll be fine. Lucy will make sure we disappear for good. I promise. Not even your family will be able to hunt me down. Wolf-y noses or not."

A clumping noise crunched on the gravel behind her.

"Are you talking to the wolf?" Lucy said, approaching the truck. She swung her way to the passenger door and maneuvered her crutches easily, tucking them in the bed of the truck before sliding onto the bench seat of the old Ford.

"Maybe."

Lucy snorted. "Well, tell him to get into the truck

bed, if he's coming."

The wolf leaped gracefully into the back of the truck as if Lucy had spoken directly to him. "Looks like he's ready," Emma said, getting into the driver's seat and starting the engine.

Emma drove slowly through town, partly because she didn't know where they were going and partly because she didn't want to accidentally send Noah flying out of the back of the truck.

Lucy directed her through the dark neighborhood and across town. They pulled to a stop in front of a small white house with a two-car detached garage, nestled at the bottom of hill between a large private driveway that led up toward a mansion and the narrow gravel road they'd been following.

A row of small wood-framed houses lined the street, aged and rustically picturesque in the moonlight, as if they'd been plucked out of an old-timey oil painting.

"What is this place? Why is there a huge house up there and small houses along the road?"

"The Stinsons built the place at the top of the hill a few years ago. They bought out a huge chunk of this neighborhood and cleared out a lot of the old houses. My little house and the others along the road are pretty much all that's left of the original neighborhood."

Lucy pointed to the detached garage building. "5-5-4-7 will open the garage door. Then we can park this truck out of sight while I get what I need from the house."

After the truck was parked and the garage door closed, Emma joined Lucy in the house with the big wolf who still refused to leave her side for even a moment. He kept sniffing the air and twitching nervously, like he was waiting for someone…or something to show up. Unfortunately the house was surrounded by woods, so sneaking up on them wasn't going to be hard.

She closed the front door behind her and blinked a few times to let her eyes adjust to the low lamplight. Lucy was nowhere in sight, but she heard clunking coming from the back of the house.

"Lucy?"

"Back here, sweetie. Come help me load this duffle bag."

Emma walked down the narrow hallway and took a left into the last bedroom.

"Can you get those smoke grenades from the basket in the corner," Lucy asked, pointing to the back of the closet.

Emma nodded and knelt down, reaching forward

and pulling the basket closer. "How many do you want?"

"Four, just to be safe. I want those guys knocked out quick. I wish we didn't have to go back to the farmhouse, but all our papers are there." Lucy tucked a large rifle into the duffle on the bed.

It was quite the stark contrast. Pink floral comforter covered by a variety of assault weapons and body armor.

"Put on one of the vests, just in case," Lucy said, pulling one over her head and then handing the other to Emma.

Emma tugged it on over her t-shirt and fastened the velcro straps so that it fit snugly to her body. She took one of the holstered handguns and pinned it to her waistband.

Flashing lights from outside and a growl from the front room made them both freeze in place.

"Does anyone know you own this house?"

Lucy shook her head. "It's owned by one of my aliases. Someone had to have reported seeing us drive by. It's a damned small town and you guys had to take a bright orange pick-up truck."

"Glad you had the garage," Emma whispered, the hairs on the back of her neck tingling as she closed her eyes and willed the cop car to keep moving. The last thing they needed was the police involved because of the stolen truck.

Emma moved toward the door of the bedroom. They should turn off the light in the front living room.

"Don't move Emma. It could cast shadows. Hopefully that oversized dog won't bark. I can feel him growling from here."

Emma's eyes widened as she realized she could indeed feel the vibrations from his growling right through the floorboards. He stopped shortly after Lucy made the comment though and Emma smiled. Even though Noah was in wolf form, he seemed to be able to understand speech the same as a human. Definite bonus for wolf-boy.

Chapter Eighteen

Hours later, Lucy and Emma had moved to the couch in the front room. No one had reported them. Up the street about a quarter mile at the top of the hill, police cars, a fire engine, and an ambulance had arrived and parked in front of the mansion.

"It's the Stinson place. The old codger must've finally died."

"That's harsh."

"He was an ass," Lucy shot back.

"Who are they?" Emma asked.

"Rich people who own half the railroads in the country. Well, his three grandsons do now, if he croaked."

Lucy continued to peer through a crack in the

curtains, cursing under her breath about people having emergencies at the worst possible times. Noah sat quietly on his haunches next to the chair Emma had curled up in. Lucy had turned off the table lamp, finally, hoping the slight movement and light going out wouldn't be noticed by any of the preoccupied emergency response teams. Now, only the light of the moon softly illuminated the room through the white curtains.

A hand touched her arm, rousing her from the drowsiness that had claimed her consciousness for a short time. Emma's eyes flew open and she straightened in the chair.

"Yes," she whispered. "Did they leave?"

"Yep, the last cop car left about ten minutes ago."

Emma unfolded her legs one at a time and stretched. The bulky vest had cut into her waist and she twisted uncomfortably, trying to stimulate blood flow to the area again.

Noah hopped to his feet, his toenails clicking softly on the hardwood floors as he paced.

"Need to go pee, wolfy?" Emma asked, a smile curving up the corners of her lips.

A deep snort erupted from the big animal and he shook his head, flapping his ears.

"Grab the duffle. Let's get out of here before someone else decides to have a heart attack tonight," Lucy said, situating herself on the crutches.

Emma slung the duffle over her shoulder and led them through the front door. Noah sprang down the steps of the porch first and trotted to the closed garage door.

A second later, a round of howls split the silent night air, prickling the hairs on the back of her neck. It sounded like a dozen wolves at least. Noah paced and whined, his dark eyes reflecting the moon as he looked back and forth from Emma to the garage.

They needed to go now. Animal or not, his warning was clear.

She hurried to the electronic panel and typed in the code. The door rolled up with only the slightest metallic squeak. Lucy tossed her crutches in the back with Noah and climbed into the driver's seat.

Emma's nerves relaxed a little more as she became a passenger for the first time since this whole debacle started. The life she'd been born into came with perks, but the cons, in her opinion, far outweighed them.

A few minutes later they were on the road again,

making their way as nonchalantly as possible across town and south to Lucy's farmhouse. It was the middle of the night and most of Somewhere was fast asleep.

"It's good it's spring break. The sheriff isn't out patrolling as much for delinquent college drunks."

"Are you out a lot at three in the morning?" Emma asked, studying the road ahead of them. They'd left the suburban area behind and were coming up on the turn-off for route 16. At least that's what the sign back a mile or so had said.

"Sometimes," Lucy said, a hint of mischief in her tone.

Emma turned to face her and frowned. "What are you doing?"

"Watching mostly. I don't like people getting to know me, but I like knowing as much as possible about everyone else."

"Stalker," Emma said under her breath.

"Yep," Lucy shot back. "I tend to do most of my shopping as close to opening or closing time as I can. Still, apparently being a single middle-aged woman in a small town automatically puts you on the radar for pastors' wives. I swear, my accident wouldn't have happened if that old bitty would mind her business and stay away from me.

Imagining the sound of her whiney nasal voice makes my skin crawl and my stomach twist."

"Geez, Lucy. Tell me how you really feel about her." Emma had to press her lips together hard to keep from grinning.

"Oh, hush. I can hear the laughter in your head, so just stop."

"I didn't think you ever let anyone get to you."

"There's always a few, Emma. You can't block out all the idiots." Lucy turned the rickety truck left onto route 16 and glanced over. "Tell me about that boy you were with. Why did he leave one of those giant hybrid dogs of theirs with you? They try to call them dogs, but I swear they run through the woods like wild animals at night."

"The nurse at the hospital said no one has ever reported them destroying property or livestock."

"Just because they aren't causing problems doesn't mean they're safe," Lucy added quickly. "And you didn't answer the question. Where did he go and why do we have his dog?"

"He said it was a family emergency and that Wolfy," Emma said, thumbing over her shoulder toward the wolf in the truck bed, "would help keep us safe."

"Wolfy? They named that monstrosity, Wolfy?"

Emma swallowed a snort. "Yes," she lied, the pitch of her voice higher than she would've preferred.

"Where did you meet Noah?"

Emma swallowed slowly and stared out into the trees before answering. "I stole his truck."

"And what? He helped you? Emma!"

"A deer or something hit my rental and it crashed near the VonBrandt gate. Well, one of them anyway. I hoofed it through one of their fields, looking for help and I kinda stumbled on an empty truck." The lie tasted like sand in her mouth, but she refused to bring Lucy in on the crazy that surrounded the VonBrandt family. It wasn't her place, anyway, and Noah trusted her not to say anything.

"So how did you meet him?" The question came again, prickling Emma's skin.

"He showed up at your house. His phone had been in the truck and he tracked it." No lies there. Noah really had tracked her using the phone tucked away in his clothing. "When Hollis and Grimes showed up, he helped me get out of there before they saw me."

"And he's been helping you since? Out of the goodness of his heart?"

Emma clasped her hand in her lap and tried to relax. "Pretty much."

"So he's hot for you?" Lucy pushed again.

"Really? You're going there?" Emma said, objecting louder than she should've.

"Why were there other people at the hospital and why wouldn't they give you your purse? Why were you running from him?"

"It's complicated, Lucy. Please drop it. We have to leave Somewhere as soon as possible."

"MmmmHmmmm." The murmur was loud enough for Lucy to get her point across without coming right out and saying "gotcha".

Chapter Nineteen

They entered Lucy's property through the stock gate she and Noah had ridden through the night before. The beginning flicker of oranges and yellows on the horizon, signaled the start of the sunrise.

Emma threw a quick glance over her shoulder. If the sunrise was supposed to affect Noah, it hadn't yet. That's all she needed. Him changing into a man—naked—in the back of the moving pick-up truck.

Lucy pulled to a stop behind a thick grove of trees and underbrush. She cut the engine, but left the keys dangling from the ignition. "When you get out, don't close the doors. The noise will carry all the way to the house when it's this quiet."

Emma nodded, leaving the door hanging after slipping out. She grabbed the duffle from the bed and heaved it over the side. The gear hit the ground with a metallic thud.

"What do you want first?" Emma asked, yanking the zipper on the bag open. A smorgasbord of weapons clinked against each other, sleek metal shining in the dawning light.

Lucy leaned against the side of the truck. "Hand me the Barrett XM 500 sniper and that scope, there," she answered, pointing toward a snazzy thermal scope. "You take the SIG, and the other Barrett rifle."

Emma pulled the rifle strap over her head and shoulder, rotating it until it rested on her back. Then took the holstered SIG and clipped it to the waistband of her pants.

"I need the knapsack of smokers, too."

Emma grabbed the small nylon backpack and handed it to Lucy, who slung it over one shoulder while she peered through the trees toward the farmhouse."

"They still there?"

"Yep," Lucy answered. "Two heat signatures."

"Are you going to be able to move okay without crutches?"

Lucy stepped forward on her boot-casted foot and nodded her head. "I'll be fine. The drugs that were making me wobbly are out of my system and the break wasn't that bad…Is that truck of Noah's still in my barn?"

"Yes," Emma said, zipping the duffle closed and slinging it over her other shoulder.

"Good. I want you to head to the barn after I throw the grenades. Disable the GPS like I taught you and put the weapons in the backseat. We'll put the jerk wads in the bed of the truck and hightail it."

Reality struck like the butt of a rifle to her face. They were leaving.

Soon.

Within a few hours she and Lucy would disappear from the country, and she'd never see Noah again. Her chest tightened painfully and she drew in a deep breath.

She glanced over at Noah, who was sitting on his haunches silently watching them both, and then trained her eye on Lucy as she stealthily approached the farmhouse, moving as if she wasn't hindered at all by a giant strap-on boot.

"Come on," Emma said, her voice barely above a whisper. The wolf moved soundlessly at her side as she made her way through the trees, snapping twigs left and right, toward the barn. It'd been a while since she'd played war games with Lucy. Her stealth approach could use some practice.

Once inside the barn, Emma moved slowly through the shadows to the driver's side door. She pulled the handle, opened the door slowly, and jumped into Noah's truck. The overhead light came to life, illuminating the cab. She pushed a small device into the 12v plug on the dashboard. The light on the jammer flashed red for a few seconds and then green.

Signal blocked. They could now use the truck without anyone being able to lo-jack them and follow.

A low howl from outside the barn made Emma's skin tingle. She slipped down from the truck's driver's seat. Noah was still in wolf form, standing a mere few feet from her.

"What is it, Noah?" she asked, pulling the SIG from her holster.

Noah nudged her leg and whined, looking from her to the raised weapon.

Guilt crept into her mind. These weren't just wolves. They were family members. She holstered the gun. "I'm not letting them take me, Noah."

The barn door slid open a few inches more and

two wolves, bigger than Noah entered, their teeth bared. One was nearly solid black and the other was a mixture of gray and white. If they hadn't been snarling in her direction, she would've called them beautiful.

Noah advanced, his hackles raised as much as the other two. Emma reached for her gun, but hesitated. She didn't know where she could shoot a wolf and not mortally wound it. What if it was his brother? Or father.

No one moved for what seemed like ages. Sweat beaded on Emma's forehead. She could hear shouting from the house and the sound of glass breaking. Lucy was moving forward, taking her house back from Hollis and Grimes. She should be helping her, not stuck here playing checkmate with a pack of wolves.

She edged closer to a side door and all three wolves mirrored her movements. The two at the door moved closer and Noah kept his shoulder pressed against her thigh. The rumble of his growl vibrated through her entire body. Instead of causing more tension, she could feel her body relaxing, knowing he was right there, ready and able to protect and stand up for her even against his family's wishes.

A sliver of sunlight snaked through the boards of the old barn and two of them began to shift. The very naked, very large man next to the door was older and unfamiliar. The other wolf sprinted out the barn door.

Noah finished shifting and pulled open the back door of his truck, grabbing from a stash of clothes in the back seat. He slipped into a pair of sweats and moved to stand in front of Emma.

"You're going to have to get in my truck and leave before Allan knocks me out."

"What?" she squeaked.

"I can't hold him off for long. He's older and better at fighting than me. I won't last very long." He turned, grabbing her shoulders and meeting her gaze. His blue eyes flashed with determination.

He was fighting for her.

"The spell," she said, her voice a breath of a whisper. "Say the spell, Noah."

"Noooooo!" Allan roared, running across the barn toward them, holding a horse blanket around his waist like a towel. "Noah. You don't want to do this!"

"It can't be undone, Emma." Noah stared at her questioningly. "You belong to me if I do this. We will always be connected in more ways than you can imagine."

"I know."

"Chun tú Geallaim mo chroí agus anam go deo," he spoke quietly, pulling her into a tight embrace. *"Chun tú Geallaim mo chroí agus anam go deo."*

Emma gasped as something intangible surrounded her. It felt like a blanket of static electricity at first, prickling and sparking, and then more like a heat wave as it melted into her skin. Emotions surged through her. Excitement. Arousal. Desire. Fear. Uncertainty. They all rioted inside her mind fighting to be heard like an angry crowd. What had he done to her? She couldn't explain what she felt. But it terrified her as much as it excited her.

"You're an idiot. You can't do this, Noah. She doesn't belong here. She won't stay with you. Your mother is going to have my head over this," Allan shouted angrily from a few feet away.

"Uncle. It's my choice. My mother knows that. I refuse to let my father "fix" my mistake by punishing Emma," Noah snarled over his shoulder.

"How could you give up your only chance at a bond for someone like this? She's the daughter of an arms dealer masquerading as a philanthropist. The pack can't take the kind of scrutiny she would bring to this town if she—Arrrrrruuuugh!"

Emma and Noah both whirled to see Kara standing over Allan's barely covered twitching body.

"Hey guys," she said, her voice much too perky for the situation. A broad smile split her face with a look of satisfaction that said she'd done something she'd really enjoyed. "I hope I wasn't interrupting. Emma, I figured you'd want your purse. And this," she said, holding up the stun gun she'd used to knock the giant deputy sheriff on his ass. "He won't be down long. I recommend moving out quickly. Your aunt has a couple of thugs hogtied on her porch."

"Crap!"

Everything had happened so quickly, she'd completely forgotten that Lucy was taking down Hollis and Grimes a few dozen yards away in the house.

Noah grabbed her arm and pulled her close, crushing his mouth to hers. She sighed and found her body melting into his before a loud growl from the ground startled her out of the blissful bubble his kiss had provided.

"I have to deal with my family. I'll find you afterward, I promise."

Her voice choked in her throat. She couldn't tell him. It hurt too much. She could feel his attraction. His desire. His genuine concern, even… love.

He pulled her wrists to his mouth and kissed the pulse point of each.

Her eyes widened as a shimmering emerald green band manifested, encircling not only her pale wrists but his tanned ones as well. This was more real than she had imagined. He'd given her more than she should've asked for. Tears welled in her eyes and she bit her lip, trying to keep them from cascading down her cheeks like fiery stripes of pain.

"Hurry," Kara said, breaking the moment between them.

Emma wiped her eyes and pulled away from Noah. Their gaze met for another second and she saw the moment he realized she wasn't coming back. Her heart felt his break, but he didn't protest. He didn't call her out on it. Instead, he walked away.

She didn't understand how this exchange worked. Hell. She didn't understand how he was a werewolf either. But this. This was hell on earth. If she could feel his heart. His pain and grief. He could feel hers, too. Her guilt. Her anguish over the choice she was making. It was like his uncle warned. If she stayed, the consequences would be catastrophic for Noah and his family.

It would never work.

Chapter Twenty

Emma turned the ignition and gassed the truck. It lurched forward and she maneuvered out of the barn. Kara had left it open more than wide enough for the truck to get through.

She swerved and headed for the back porch, stopping where Lucy was standing over two crumpled bodies. Hollis and Grimes had definitely had better days.

"What took you so long? Help me get them into the bed of the truck."

Emma jumped out, surprised by Lucy's ability to dead lift an unconscious man. "What are we doing with them?"

"Leaving them at the sheriff's office on our way out of town."

"What's he going to do with them? Their covers will show in the system."

Lucy shook her head as they slammed the tailgate closed. "I hacked their covers and fixed that problem. When the sheriff runs their prints, they will go directly to jail for the rest of their miserable lives. No one messes with my little girl and gets away with it."

Emma grimaced, feeling the slightest bit of pity for the two mercenaries in the back of the truck.

"I'll drive, sweetheart. Grab those go-bags I packed us," she said, pointing to the porch again.

She hurried around the side of the truck and took the stairs onto the porch two at a time. Grabbing the duffles, she hurried to the truck, nerves sailing toward red-alert freak-out-mode when another truck pulled around the side of the house. She recognized Aaron VonBrandt and his wife from the other night.

Tossing the bags into the back seats, she scrambled into the cab and slammed the door behind her. "We have to go, now!"

"Why are the VonBrandts on my property? What is going on between you and them? And when the hell did you have time to get tattoos?"

"Lucy," she hissed. "Floor it."

The truck surged forward and seconds later they were flying toward town. It took them only a few minutes to reach the sheriff's station and the dark front windows of the street were a clear indication that no one was awake or open yet.

"Are you going to tell me why the VonBrandts are hunting you like a pack of wolves?"

Words of surprise leapt to her tongue, but she held them back. Lucy didn't know. She couldn't know. "It's complicated and I'd rather not talk about it."

"Fair enough. That boy knows we are leaving, right?"

"He knows," Emma whispered.

Lucy pulled to a stop in front of the sheriff's office and left the truck idling.

Emma got out and together they moved both men to the sidewalk next to the sheriff's front door. Lucy injected the unconscious men with something, and then handcuffed them to the bike rack that was bolted into the concrete sidewalk.

They turned to go to the truck and froze in place. A man stood across the street, leaning against a telephone pole, staring. His wide-brimmed hat was pulled down to cover most of his face and he wore typical clothes for being in a small Texas town —

jeans, flannel shirt, boots. But the way he watched them made Emma's inner cop radar buzz frantically.

Lucy saw him too. Emma had seen the hitch in her step when she turned around, and it wasn't the heavy-booted broken foot. He didn't move toward them or say anything. The staring match only lasted a few seconds before Lucy started for the driver's seat. Emma followed suit.

"Do you know him?" Emma asked, as they turned the corner and left the sheriff's office in the rearview mirror.

"Nope, he's new in town. A nice-looking man built like a brick house and taller than sin-on-steroids doesn't go unnoticed in Somewhere."

"Lucy."

"What? I might be old, but I'm never gonna be old enough not to appreciate a handsome man."

Emma let the sigh she'd been holding onto slip slowly from her lungs. A few more turns had them barreling out of town and toward the highway. A sign for Houston appeared shortly after getting onto the busy four-lane freeway.

Each mile made the hole in Emma's heart grow bigger. Noah's anguish choked the air from her lungs and tore tore a hole in her heart. She'd hurt him—deeply. Except… it hurt her as much as it did him. Everything he felt she could feel. The farther they got, the more it felt like the drive was literally going to rip her heart, or her soul, from her chest.

She glanced down at her wrists again. Two wide green bands of Celtic knots encircled them, and strands from one circlet intertwined with the other, like a plant that had grown roots alongside another plant.

He'd had them too. The markings on his wrists had been nearly identical, only wider and more pronounced, like a male and female version of the same thing. Where hers were delicate and feminine, his had been darker and the strands had been wider.

"What are the tattoos?" Lucy asked, moving to the left lane of the highway.

"A memory."

"Of Noah?"

Emma nodded. "Yes."

"I've seen tattoos like that before. Lots of the VonBrandts have them, usually only paired off ones though. You didn't marry that boy or anything crazy, did you?"

"No," Emma said, "Nothing crazy." Which was the furthest thing from the truth. But she couldn't talk to Lucy about the VonBrandts. It was their secret, and she'd promised Noah she would carry it. Though now it was her secret as well.

"Are we going to Houston?"

"We will pass through it. We'll stop for the night in San Antonio, then head to Laredo where I have a contact who can get us through the border into Mexico without a hitch."

"Will we stay in Mexico?"

"Yes, I have a safe house on the coast of Argentina. We'll head to it and we can get your family finances in order from there."

"I'll never be able to go home, will I?"

"No, sweetie. Not to the Hamptons. People will be watching for that. But eventually you'll be able to return to the states. We will need to make sure your new identity is solid. Change your hair color a little. But you'll never be able to go back to your old life. To old friends."

Emma swallowed. A new wave of grief washed over her. She might not have lost her memories to some spell, but she was still losing everything about her life. She was still being forced to start over completely.

"It's going to be okay, sweetheart. I promise. Life will eventually seem more normal. Give it time." Lucy's voice held a shadow of promise. She wouldn't lie to her. She'd never lied to her. If she thought things would get better, then Emma trusted that they would. She wished she didn't have an invisible dagger plunged into her chest that drove a little deeper with each mile of highway they put between them and Somewhere. She'd couldn't imagine how much it was going to hurt when they made it all the way to Mexico…all the way to the coast.

Chapter Twenty-One

Noah sat against one of the center posts of Lucy's barn. After he'd said the spell, everything between them had become so transparent. He could feel her attraction and her hesitation. They were both drawn to each other, but she was running from something terrible. A darkness that threatened to completely envelop her. Something that frightened her enough to leave town without saying goodbye—even though they were completely bonded. The pull between them was strong. Leaving, had not been easy. Still, it afforded little comfort.

She'd still left.

His mate.

The woman his wolf had sensed had left him.

He'd seen the bond in her eyes after their kiss in

the barn and felt the hole in his soul widen when she'd driven out of town. He rubbed his wrists where the intricate tattoos wound their connected patterns. Their bond solidified instantly. He hadn't realized it would. But he should've. They'd already slept together.

The emotional and physical connection had struck like a bolt of lightning.

His parents had yelled for a few minutes, until they noticed the bands on his wrists. Then they did their best to comfort him. Offer him some kind of hope for the future. But he had none without her. He'd known she might leave, but he hadn't realized how painful it was to be so far from her. The further she traveled, the harder it was to maintain the connection between them. He was losing her.

His father and uncles had done their best to reach out and find her with contacts above and under the board. To no avail. It was as if she'd literally dropped off the face of the earth.

Allan said it was called going off grid.

Day after day, Noah found himself back in old lady Craig's barn. He could still catch Emma's scent here. It was the only place in town he could still find it.

He took a deep breath and looked up at the glints

of sun shining through the walls of the old barn. Old hay, manure, and a little of her clung in the air. It was almost gone now. Soon he wouldn't be able to connect with her here either.

Then it would get really bad.

The only place he found respite from the pain was in his books. Literature and history were his refuge. He'd thrown himself into his studies and gotten A's in everything. Even in the math class he despised.

"Noah?" His brother's voice pierced the early morning silence. Finals were over now.

"I'm here," he said, his voice thick with emotion. He wiped his eyes in case an unwelcome tear showed itself.

The door on the barn creaked and Luke slipped inside, sinking to the floor of the barn on the opposite side of the post, putting them back to back.

"How did you know I was here?" Noah asked, leaning his head against his arms as he draped them over his raised knees.

"Mom called and said you never came down for breakfast. This is where we always find you when you disappear early in the morning."

"You've been following me?"

"Yep." Luke chuckled. "Mom wanted to know you were okay."

"You mean she wanted to be sure I hadn't left."

"That too," Luke said, his voice low and drawn out. "You have to go find her, Noah. You can't live like this."

Noah sighed. If only it were that easy. Maybe, if he had followed her from the very start, but now…now he would wander forever, always trying to get a bead on her location. The pain of losing her overwhelmed the beacon he should be able to use to track her.

"If she needed or wanted me half as much as I do her. She would come back."

"You know that's not true. You told me she was afraid. She's staying away to protect you. She's probably curled up somewhere just as miserable as you are, dreaming of seeing your ugly face again."

"Hey, at least I don't have yours." Noah raised his head and felt his lips twitch as a smile played with the corners.

He missed his twin brother. They might not have identical faces, but their personalities were more alike than either of them cared to admit, even though their interests varied greatly. He missed living with him.

"I don't know where to start. It's been too long. I can't feel her anymore."

"That's hogwash and you know it." Luke snorted. "Close your eyes, find her scent, and slow your heart."

"How do you know what to do?"

"I asked Dad."

"He wants me to find her?" Noah sat up straight and twisted to the side so that he now faced Luke.

"They want you to be happy. I told them the only way that would happen is if you found Emma and brought her back to Somewhere. She hasn't returned to the Hamptons or popped up anywhere else. Allan has been keeping an ear to the ground and Uncle Jason said a lawyer buddy of his told him that last week the Carrington estate was finalized and liquidated."

Noah shook his head. She would've come back to him. Wouldn't she? If she was free of the darkness that plagued her, he would've felt her relief. Or was he too much of a mess to feel anything right now?

"Are you ready to try? Or do you want to sit in this musty old barn and hope for the best while your life with Emma fades into the aether? Even Kara, has been bugging me about it."

Noah took another deep breath and glanced

toward the barn door. "Tell me what to do. The last thing I need is your girlfriend giving me a guilt trip. If she's bugging you, I know I'm next on the list, especially since I can smell her standing outside."

His brother smiled. "I wondered how long it would take you to realize she came with me."

"Her scent is all over you, but the breeze started to carry it through the cracks in the walls."

Luke stood and Noah followed suit.

"Dad said to close your eyes and picture her in your mind. Slow your pulse and take long deep breaths."

Noah followed his brother's directions. When his eyes closed, he could see her as she'd been last— about to cry as she left him right where he was standing. Pain lanced through his heart like a knife and a tear rolled down his cheek.

"Push past that memory and look for her. Your souls are tied together. You can find her. Search for that strong connection you had those first few days. Pull it forward."

That connection to her was tangible after the initial spell had been cast. For the first few days, he'd known exactly where she was and could almost hear the roar of the truck engine and the jolt as the raced down the highways away from him. He'd felt the warm breeze on her cheek the day after she left, like she was outside somewhere standing in the sun. And he'd felt the burn of tears when she'd cried herself to sleep that first night.

He should've followed her then, but he was angry and hurt. She'd been able to ignore the call of their bond and leave him behind. He should be able to do the same.

He'd fled the house after feeling her sorrow. Turning into a wolf the second his feet touched the ground outside. He ran until his lungs gave out and he collapsed onto a bed a prickly needles at the base of a large grove of old pines.

But then he'd felt her fear and confusion. She'd felt him running. She could feel everything he felt. So he'd shut it off. He'd blocked everything so she could have peace...so he could try to do the same.

It hadn't worked.

Now he had to flip the switch again and feel all of her rushing back into his consciousness. She wouldn't be able to block him. She hadn't been taught how.

He had to find the thread.

It was there in the back of his mind. He could feel the power ebbing and flowing through it. Pulling it forward, he focused on it and felt the magick grow and expand as it came rushing back. It hadn't been as hard as he thought it would be, but it was much more painful.

He groaned and leaned forward, resting his shoulder against the post. She was there in his mind once again. He could feel heat from the sun. She was sad, but not distraught. Her pulse was speeding up. He knew she could feel the bridge between them unfurling again. It had to be so confusing. Soon he would explain everything and she would be safe in his arms again. Soon this pain would be gone.

Whatever had driven her away from him the first time didn't matter anymore. He would face anything to have her again. He just needed her to feel the same way.

"I love you, Emma. I'm coming for you."

"You found her?"

Noah nodded. "Tell Dad to call the airport. I'm going to need the plane."

Chapter Twenty-Two

"Emma."

"Out here, Lucy," Emma called from the veranda of their small villa in Argentina. It was on the side of a mountain, looking out over the small town below. It was a quiet place to disappear. That's what they'd done—completely disappear.

It had been necessary. People were hunting her. One by one, Lucy had made sure they were taken care of—arrested or...something else. But after things calmed down, she missed her life. But mostly she missed Noah. Which was stupid in her mind, because she barely knew him.

Yet, there was this magickal connection they had. She'd felt it right after he'd said the spell in the barn and then for nearly a week afterward. Every breath of pain and anguish he'd felt, she'd felt. How, she didn't know. But somehow something was allowing her to feel his emotions. Even sometimes to feel things physically that he was feeling.

Then one day it stopped.

And Noah's absence left an emptiness in her that made her weep. It was like he'd cut the cord. Everything was gone. The feelings. The sense of being connected. It was all gone. She was alone. Weeks passed before she was able to stop begging Lucy to take her back to Somewhere, Texas. She had to see him again. At least to know he was alive and well. Not knowing if something had happened to him was worse torture than sharing his pain had ever been.

But then three days ago, the connection came back. It was different this time. Stronger and swelled with a confidence that hadn't been there previously. The pain had been replaced with hope.

She spent every day on the veranda, watching the road, waiting for him to appear. His presence got stronger and stronger, until every nerve ending in her body hummed with anticipation. She needed to see him as much as touch him. Taste him.

"He's coming, isn't he?" Lucy walked up and stopped next to her chair.

"I have to go with him, Lucy. I love him. I can't explain it, but I do and I have to, Lu—"

"Shhhhh, child. I understand. There are only a few people left that present you any threat at all and none of them will think to look for you in Somewhere. But you will have to keep a low profile and you won't be able to contact your old friends again. You'll also have to keep your alias. You can never officially be a Carrington again."

Emma smiled. "I like being Emma Craig. I'm fine with living a different life, Lucy. I just…"

"I know." Lucy turned to leave, but paused. "I'll give you two some privacy."

"You know he's almost here? How?" Emma asked, her eyes searching the road again.

"A friend called me when he landed at the airport," Lucy answered, a hint of amusement in her eyes. "I know almost everything before it happens."

Emma grinned. "I think you're the one who might need to relax a little more."

"Never happen," Lucy said as she left the porch and disappeared into the villa.

No. It probably wouldn't.

The rumble of an engine on the road snagged her attention and she stood from her chair. A brown jeep pulled up to the front of the house. Noah's tousled light brown hair was flipping in the wind, begging for her fingers to dig through it. She met his heated blue gaze and leapt from the porch to the driveway below.

"Emma." He slipped from the Jeep, his black cowboy boots hitting the gravel drive with a crunch.

She was in his arms before he could take another step. Their emotions swirled around them. Fear. Love. Joy. Anxiety. It was a mix of long overdue excitement and nervousness about what the other might say.

His strong arms encircled her and she took a deep breath of the woodsy piney scent still clinging to his blue plaid flannel shirt. Soft, yet deliciously strong and masculine. She'd missed him so much.

"God, I love you, Emma." He squeezed her tighter and buried his face in her hair. "You have to come home with me. I need you more than the air I'm breathing right now. I know you can feel it, too. I know it's confusing and frightening and I'm sorry I didn't have time to explain everything that would happen. But, I want that chance now. Please, Emma. Just give me a chance."

"I want that, too, Noah. I want you with every breath I take. With every beat of my heart, I ache to be with you." Emma slid her hands up his hard chest to his neck and then cupped his scratchy face. His love for her poured out of him and into her like water flowing from a fountain, washing away any doubt she'd ever had about staying with him.

"Lucy said it's okay for me to go. But I have to keep my true identity a secret."

"Whatever it is that haunts you, I can protect you. My family can protect you. You are family. You are mine," he said, the last part only a whisper as he slipped his hand into her hair and pulled her mouth to meet his.

His lips crushed hers and she melted into his kiss. Feeling the rush of emotions flow between them was heady.

Nothing had ever felt more perfect. More right.

No one had ever felt more like home.

She pulled back and cupped his face. His blue eyes pierced her soul. Magic may have sealed the bond, but she'd fallen for him long before that spell had been cast.

"I love you too, Noah."

About The Author

Krystal Shannan goes to sleep every night dreaming of mythical realms with werewolves, vampires, fae, and dragons. Occasionally a fabulous, completely human story slips into the mix, but powers and abilities usually crop up without fail, twisting reality into whatever her mind can conceive.

As a child, her parents encouraged her interests in Ancient Greek and Roman mythology and all things historical and magickal. As an adult, the interests only grew. She is a child of Neverland and refuses to ever stop believing in fairies. She is guilty of indulging in and being a Buffy the Vampire Slayer groupie as well as an Angel fan. For those of you unfamiliar with the world of Joss Whedon, you are missing out!

She also makes sure to watch as many action and adventure movies as possible. The more exciting the better. Yippee-Ki-Yay..... If you don't know the end of that phrase, then you probably don't like the same movies.

Printed in Great Britain
by Amazon